He wasn't prepared for what he saw.

She was sitting at her desk—a slender blonde whose every movement promised curves that would melt a man's knees even as it brought him down to them.

The source of his sister's ire looked up at him with the clearest bluest eyes he'd ever seen. The word *beautiful* pushed its way through the sudden cobwebs that had taken Paul's brain hostage. It took him a moment to realize that he wasn't breathing.

He stopped to breathe.

She did not look like someone who was hired to do battle with mudslingers. She looked more like a fairy-tale princess who had sprung from someone's smitten fantasy.

Dear Reader,

I love babies. I always have, always will. Unlike a lot of my friends, I had absolutely no trouble getting pregnant. I also know, much to the embarrassment of my children, exactly when each of them was conceived.

Since holding my newborns in my arms and being a mom is something I cannot imagine not being part of my life, I can completely understand how the Armstrong Fertility Institute could be perceived as a beacon of hope to childless couples. This is the first book in a six-book series about the institute and the people who are a part of helping to make the miracle of birth happen for couples desperate to have a baby. But along with the miracles come secrets and intrigue.... I hope that this book and the books that follow will entertain you.

Thank you for reading, and as ever, I wish you someone to love who loves you back.

Wishing you all the best,

Marie Ferrarella

PRESCRIPTION FOR ROMANCE

MARIE FERRARELLA

SPECIAL EDITION®

Published by Silhouette Books

America's Publisher of Contemporary Romance

Special thanks and acknowledgment to Marie Ferrarella for her contribution to THE BABY CHASE miniseries.

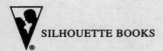

SILHOUETTE BOOKS

Recycling programs
for this product may
not exist in your area.

ISBN-13: 978-0-373-65499-4

PRESCRIPTION FOR ROMANCE

Visit Silhouette Books at www.eHarlequin.com

Printed in U.S.A.

Books by Marie Ferrarella

MARIE FERRARELLA

This *USA TODAY* bestselling and RITA® Award-winning author has written almost two hundred novels for Silhouette Books, some under the name Marie Nicole. Her romances are beloved by fans worldwide. Visit her Web site at www.marieferrarella.com.

To
Jessica and Nicholas
with all my love forever,
Mom

Chapter One

Dr. Paul Armstrong was deeply concerned.

His sister Olivia Armstrong Mallory could have never, by any stretch of the imagination, been described as robust or even glowingly healthy, but she sat in his office today, turning to him not just as her older brother, but as the chief of staff of the Armstrong Fertility Institute. He knew talking about this wasn't easy for his sister. She'd addressed half her story to the crumpled tissue she held in a death grip between her fingers in her lap.

How many times since he'd begun to work here had he heard this same story before? Too many times, and yet, not enough to become insensitive to it.

Olivia wanted to become pregnant and all her attempts, she had confided quietly, had thus far failed.

Even as he listened to her haltingly pour out her heart, Paul began to suspect that there was more to all this than she was telling him. Something beyond the hunger to have a child.

"Olivia," he pointed out gently, "you're being too hard on yourself. You're just twenty-nine—"

Eyes full of misery and unshed tears looked up at him. "And I've been trying to get pregnant for five years, Paul. Five very long, disappointing years."

This, too, he'd seen over and over again. The anguished faces of frustrated women, pleading for help, asking him to make the most natural of dreams come true for them. He'd never imagined he'd see this look on the face of one of his sisters.

"Olivia, there are other avenues. You could adopt a child," he tactfully suggested.

But he could see, even as he said it, that for Olivia, this wasn't the solution. She pressed a small, fisted hand beneath her breast, pushing against her incredibly flat belly. "I want to feel life growing inside me, Paul."

Though his heart went out to her, Paul felt bound to tell her what he told every woman or couple who came in to see him with this same dilemma. "It isn't all roses, Livy. There's a very real downside to being pregnant." Assuming, he added silently, that he could even get her there.

Olivia shook her head, her sleek black hair shadowing the adamant movement. "Don't you understand I don't care?" Reaching across the desk that separated them, his sister took his hands in hers in supplication. "I *really* want to be pregnant. Help me, Paul. Whatever it takes, help me."

The force of her words had him wondering again. He had to ask. "Olivia, is everything all right?"

Releasing his hands, his sister drew herself up in her chair as she squared her shoulders. "Everything's fine, Paul."

Her words only reinforced his concern. "You said that much too fast."

Olivia inclined her head. "All right, I'll say it slower. Every-thing's-fine." She deliberately drew out the sentence, saying it in slow motion and awarding it a host of syllables.

He would have laughed if he wasn't so concerned. "Livy, I'm your brother. You can talk to me."

"I *am* talking to you," she insisted. "I'm telling you that I want to have a baby. As the chief of staff you should be able to understand that." Blowing out a breath and clearly struggling not to cry, Olivia asked, "Now, can you help me?"

Though he had a tendency to be oblivious to the obvious at times, the irony of the situation did not escape Paul. The daughter of the famous fertility expert Dr. Gerald Armstrong was infertile. Somewhere, the gods were chuckling.

If he ever helped anyone at all, Paul thought, he should be able to help his sister.

"Yes," he answered gently, "I think there's a good chance that I can." Of late, there had been a number of allegations of wrongdoing, rumored to be made by a former disgruntled employee, of eggs and sperm being switched, research that was held suspect and too many multiple births, all of which had caused a cloud of suspicion to be cast over the institute and the work they'd done over the years. Paul had been going out of his way to try to right all of this. He began by luring the world-famous Bonner-Demetrios research team away from a prominent San Francisco teaching hospital and getting them to head up the institute's research operations here.

Just in time, he thought, looking at his sister.

"We've just scored a coup and managed to get two top-flight physicians to join our staff here. Both of them have been on the cutting edge of fertility research for some time now. I'm going to refer you to one of them."

Olivia nodded, desperately trying to draw hope from her brother's words. "What's his name?"

"Dr. Chance Demetrios. If there's any way possible for you to wind up getting morning sickness, he'll find it," Paul promised with a quick smile. Paul wrote a few words on a pad, then tore the page off and held it out to her. "I know he doesn't have patients today until later. Are you willing to go now?"

Olivia looked down at the slip of paper her brother had

given her, unable to read a single word. She sincerely hoped that another doctor would have no trouble deciphering the hieroglyphics. "Are you sure he can see me?"

Paul smiled the shy, boyish smile she remembered so well from their childhood, the smile she recalled gracing the lips of her protector. Derek, their other brother, was always the one in the foreground, gregarious, loud and charming. But it was Paul she always felt she could count on. Paul was the dependable one who spoke little, but meant every word he said.

"Yes," he assured her. "I'm his boss. Chance'll see you." Rising, he came around the desk and squeezed his sister's hand. "Sure there's nothing else you want to tell me?"

Olivia stood up and did her best to smile. "I'm sure."

That wasn't good enough for him. Paul tried again. "Maybe there's something you don't want to tell me, but should?"

"Only that I love you." Olivia rose on her toes and brushed a quick kiss to his cheek. Backing away, she held up the note he'd just given her. "Thank you."

Paul sincerely hoped that Chance was the magician the man claimed to be. "Anytime," he replied.

His sister left his office, closing the door behind her. Paul went back around to his chair.

He'd just managed to sit down when the door flew open again, this time without a perfunctory knock or even the pretense of formality. His other sister, Lisa—the head administrator at the institute—burst in with just a tiny bit less noise than a detonating cherry bomb. Ordinarily, she vacillated between looking harried and looking pleased because another happy couple had left the institute, pregnant and satisfied. Now she looked as if she was about to bite someone's head off.

"Do you know what he did?" she demanded angrily, slamming the door closed with a bang.

Paul had always found it was best to remain calm in the face of anyone's tirade. If he remained calm, he could assess the problem more accurately. "Who?" he asked mildly.

Lisa looked at him as if he'd suddenly turned simple on her. "Derek, of course."

"Of course," Paul echoed. Taking a breath, he patiently pointed something out—and not for the first time. "Lisa, contrary to legend and a handful of fair-to-bad movies, just because Derek and I are twins does *not* mean that I automatically know what he's thinking, so, no, I don't know what he did." And then he smiled indulgently at her. "But I'm sure you're going to enlighten me."

Lisa let out a loud huff and Paul would have been hard-pressed to say who she was angrier at right now, Derek or him. "He's gone off on his own, that's what he's done."

He was going to need more of a hint than that. "As in…he left?" He sincerely doubted that Derek would just run off at such a difficult time and leave his siblings to deal with the entire mess. But he had to admit that he and Derek often marched to completely different drummers and there were times when his brother's actions and motivation completely mystified him. Not only that, but of late, he seemed to be preoccupied.

"No, as in going off and hiring someone to— Now wait a sec—" Lisa held her hand up in case Paul was going to interrupt her "—I want to get this straight. 'Someone to help us *repair* our image.'" Then Lisa fisted her hands on her hips. "*I'm* head administrator here and Derek's gone and hired a PR manager without so much as saying boo to me."

Paul sighed. He lived and breathed his work to the exclusion of almost everything else, except for his family. Very seldom did he come up for air, much less to mingle in the everyday dealings of running the institute.

Paul asked his fuming sister, "What do you mean?"

"Public relations, Paul," she said, even more annoyed. "Derek went and hired a damn spin doctor."

"So what's the issue?" he asked, confused.

Lisa threw up her hands in desperation. "For such an intelligent man, you can be so dense sometimes. The point is, Derek is the chief financial officer—he isn't supposed to hire anyone without consulting us. Major positions are supposed to be filled by the three of us evaluating the candidate for the job, remember?" She didn't wait for him to respond before she went on. "If you ask me, I think Derek's beginning to envision himself as Caesar."

Lisa was the youngest and as such, she was given

to exaggeration. "Dial it down a notch, Lisa. I don't like Derek doing something like this without consulting us, either, but I think it's a stretch equating him with Julius Caesar."

"I'm not equating him with Caesar," she protested. "I think Derek *sees* himself as Caesar. The bottom line is," she said with a toss of her short black hair, "we don't need a PR manager."

Paul nodded. "At least we're in agreement about that."

It never occurred to her that Paul would see it any differently than she did. "Good, then fix it," she demanded. When he raised an inquisitive eyebrow, Lisa pressed, "Unhire her."

Even though terminating this unwanted new employee was his first inclination, Paul did want to be fair. That would mean talking to Derek and finding out just what his brother was thinking when he hired this person. "Where's Derek now?"

Lisa sighed. "I have no idea. You know how he is, social butterflying all over. But I *do* know where the new girl is," she said triumphantly. "She's in Connie Winston's old office," she said, referring to a recently retired officer of their board of directors. Lisa was clearly not finished with the topic. "You know, Derek's got no right to constantly usurp us like that."

Paul had always been ready to go the extra mile, giving everyone the benefit of the doubt. "Derek probably doesn't even realize that's what he's doing. You know he gets impatient when things don't go as fast as he thinks they should." Paul shrugged philosophically. "He doesn't have the patience of a scientist."

Lisa pounced on her brother's words. "Good thing you do. Now get rid of this woman and give Derek a piece of your mind when you find him."

He laughed, shaking his head. "If I gave all the people who I think deserve it a piece of my mind, I wouldn't have any mind left to use for myself."

Lisa's frown was back. "So then you're not going to tell Derek that he's got to stop making unilateral decisions?"

"I didn't say that, did I?" His eyes held hers until Lisa shook her head. "I'll talk to Derek," he told her, then added, "not that I think it'll do any good."

"You're probably right," she was forced to agree. "But you never know, maybe we'll get lucky. But first," she emphasized, "you have to give that woman her walking papers."

There were times when Lisa was like a hungry dog with a bone. She just wouldn't let go. Which meant he'd get no peace until he gave in. Paul rose again. "Connie Winston's old office, you said?"

Lisa nodded. "The three of us are supposed to be running this clinic. It's the Armstrong Fertility Institute, not Derek Armstrong's Fertility Institute. If anything, it should be Dad's name, not Derek's."

Paul put his hands on his sister's arms, trying to settle her before she got riled up again.

"Take a deep breath, Lisa—and calm down. There

are a hell of a lot worse things going on in the world. Derek playing king is really just small potatoes in comparison."

"Emperor," Lisa corrected doggedly.

He closed his eyes for a moment. He was *not* going to get sidelined with semantics. "Whatever."

Paul was fully aware that if he even attempted to put off this woman's termination, Lisa would continue bedeviling him until such time as he would make good on his promise. His sister meant well, he thought, but she tended to get far too worked up. Still, she was right. Derek shouldn't have just gone off and hired someone without even running the idea past them. This was a completely new post his brother had created.

Did they really need someone to try to restore the institute's good name? Or rather, their father's good name even though it wasn't imprinted on the front of the building?

Dr. Gerald Armstrong had always been a little larger than life when it came to the public eye. Paul was not ashamed to say that he revered his father and the groundbreaking work he had done. He'd gotten away from the boy he had once been. The boy who, when he was growing up, felt his father was accessible to everyone but his own family. He knew his mother felt that. Gerald Armstrong was always far too busy making a name for himself to enjoy the name he had already gotten, almost by accident: Dad.

Still, that was all water under the bridge now. A

man was what he was and Gerald Armstrong was an excellent physician, a visionary and the last hope for a great many women who had been told that they would never be able to hold a child of their own in their arms.

The rest of it—the feet of clay, the women, the pre-occupation—well, that could all be forgiven, Paul thought, walking down the corridor to the office where, according to his sister, he would find his brother's latest mistake—and it really was a mistake, in Paul's opinion. Right now, they needed every last penny to be spent on research, not "spin." The research team he'd lured away from San Francisco did *not* come cheaply.

Approaching the until recently evacuated office, Paul knocked on the door, then knocked again when he received no answer. He was about to try again when a melodious voice told him to, "Come in." Apparently the focus of his sister's ire was indeed in.

He wasn't good at firing people. Actually, to his rec-ollection, he never had. He'd always been satisfied with the people he'd selected. There was no need to fire any of them.

Twisting the knob, he opened the door and walked in, not knowing what to expect.

He wasn't prepared for what he saw.

She was sitting at her desk, a slender blonde whose every movement promised curves that would melt a man's knees. She looked up at him with the clearest, bluest eyes he'd ever seen. The word *beautiful* pushed its way through the sudden cobwebs that had taken his brain hostage. It took him a moment to realize that he wasn't breathing.

She did not look like someone who was hired to do battle with mudslingers. She looked more like a fairy-tale princess who had sprung up from someone's smitten fantasy.

The woman seemed to light up as she saw who was walking into her office. Her face became a wreath of smiles.

"Mr. Armstrong, hello." The young woman half rose in her seat, as if she was eagerly ready to hop to do his bidding at the slightest suggestion. "What can I do for you, sir?"

Bracing himself, Paul said in his kindest voice—because it wasn't in him to be cruel—"I'm afraid you're going to have to pack up your things and leave."

The smile on her perfect face faded, replaced by bewilderment. "Excuse me?"

He hated this, he thought. He tried again, sounding even more gentle than before. "I think there's been a mistake." Each word felt more awkward on his tongue than the last. This was *definitely* not his forte. "I mean, we really don't need a public relations person."

The woman was obviously not going to go quietly. "But you just hired me," she protested with feeling.

She didn't look angry, he thought, which surprised him. What she looked like was someone who was set to dig in. She still thought she was dealing with his brother, Paul realized. He needed to set her straight before he continued.

"No, I didn't," he began, but got no further in his explanation.

"Yes, you did," she insisted. "Yesterday. We were in your office and you distinctly said you were hiring me." Her blue eyes seemed intense as she peered at his face. "Is something wrong?" she wanted to know. "I haven't done anything yet, much less something that would make you want to fire me."

"I don't want to fire you," Paul said and it was true. "I wouldn't have hired you in the first place—"

"But you did," she reminded him with feeling.

"No, I didn't," Paul told her again. "That was my brother."

Her eyes narrowed and the frown on her face told him she wasn't buying it.

"Your evil twin?" she asked with more than a tiny trace of sarcasm in her voice.

Finally, Paul thought. "Actually, I don't generally think of him in that light, but now that you mention it, yes."

The young woman stared at him as if he'd lost his mind. "Excuse me?"

Any breakthrough he'd thought had been made faded like dancing dandelion seeds in the warm spring breeze. "Maybe I should explain—"

He could see that she was struggling to remain civil. Looking at it from her point of view, he couldn't blame her.

"Maybe you should," she agreed.

Chapter Two

Bravado was second nature to Ramona Tate. It always had been. Her chosen field of investigative reporting had only honed that ability. She could bluff her way through practically everything.

Because she had never gone through an ugly-duckling stage and had been a swan from the moment she came into the world, Ramona had to constantly keep proving herself. People naturally assumed that a) because she was beautiful, that meant she didn't have a brain in her head, and b) she'd gotten to her present stage in life because she'd slept her way there.

In both cases, nothing could have been further from the truth.

Blessed with a near-genius IQ, Ramona still had to work twice as hard as the next person to be taken seriously and to keep from being dismissed as "just another empty-headed pretty face." This while politely, but deftly and succinctly, putting men in their place if they decided to become too familiar with her. In the latter case, whenever "hands-on" experience was mentioned, her antennae instantly went up because most of the men she'd encountered took that to mean their "hands on" her body.

Ramona always made it perfectly clear that working and playing well with others did not refer to the kind of playing that could be done beneath the sheets. She fought her own battles and protected her private life—what there was of it—zealously.

Since wrongdoing on any level was something she abhorred, Ramona found that she took to investigative reporting like the proverbial duck to water. Even at her seemingly tender age of twenty-five, she had already broken a number of stories, revealing fraudulent practices at one of the country's larger life insurance companies, and exposing a doctor who had made a career out of bilking Medicare, submitting charges for the treatment of nonexistent conditions for nonexistent patients in order to collect Medicare's payments. Both stories had necessitated her going undercover to get the information she needed to substantiate her allegations.

Ramona had followed the same path here, at the Armstrong Fertility Institute. Once revered as a bastion of hope for the terminally infertile, the institute's outstanding success rate had bred a certain amount of envy, which begged for closer scrutiny. This scrutiny in turn gave birth to ugly rumors, some that were quite possibly well founded, others that almost certainly were not.

That was going to be her job—to separate fact from fiction, no matter how deeply the former appeared to be buried.

But Ramona had a far more personal reason to have gone undercover at the institute. She needed to gain access to the institution's older records in hopes of saving her mother's life. Her mother, who had raised Ramona by herself, had been diagnosed with leukemia less than six months ago. The prognosis was not good. If something wasn't done soon to stem its course, her mother had only a very short time to live.

Katherine Tate desperately needed a bone-marrow transplant. Ramona would have gladly given up hers. She would have given her mother any organ she could to save the woman's life, but, as happened all too frequently, her marrow wasn't a match. So the search was on for some miscellaneous stranger whose marrow might provide the cure.

There was, however, a glimmer of hope when Ramona remembered accidentally stumbling over a piece of vital information packed away in a long-forgotten box hidden in the back of her closet.

Katherine Tate was one of those people who never threw anything away, she just moved it around every so often from one pile to another, from one room to another. In one of her many, *many* boxes throughout the house was a bundle of receipts and bills dating back more than a couple of decades. Including a receipt from the Armstrong Fertility Institute for the purchase of donor eggs.

In between jobs and desperate for money, Katherine had sold a part of herself in order that "some poor childless couple know the kind of joy I do." At least, those had been her mother's words when Ramona had finally confronted Katherine with her find.

Now Ramona could only hope that the eggs had been used and that somewhere out there she had a sibling walking around. A sibling whose bone marrow would turn out to be a perfect match for her mother.

Finding this sibling was far more important to Ramona than breaking the story of any ethical wrongdoing on the institute's part.

But she wouldn't be able to do either if this bipolar man made good on his threat to terminate her before she even got started in her search. For that to happen, she needed to get entrenched here. She already knew that calling the institute's administration office with her plight was an exercise in futility. When she had, the woman on the other end of the line had briskly told her that accessing the old records would be a violation of those patients' right to privacy.

Yeah, right. As if the Armstrongs and their minions actually cared a fig about doing the right thing.

"You were hired," Paul began slowly, trying to carefully hit all the salient points, "by someone who didn't have the proper authority to hire anyone by himself."

Ramona felt her temper shortening.

"I don't understand," she said, hoping that the smile on her lips didn't look as fake as it felt to her.

Paul backtracked in his head, realizing that he'd failed to state the most obvious part, the part that would instantly untangle the rest. Or so he hoped.

"You see, I'm twins."

She stared at him, her blue eyes widening. "You are?"

That sounded stupid, he upbraided himself. "I mean, I'm one of twins. I have a brother," he told her. "He looks just like me. His name's Derek and *he's* the one who hired you."

Her expression never changed, but her tone was slightly incredulous as she asked, "You're not Derek Armstrong?"

Finally. The light at the end of the tunnel was beginning to materialize, he thought, relieved. "No, I'm Paul."

Twins. Damn, how had she missed that? She'd been so consumed with getting ammunition against the institute and being angry because they wouldn't just help her get at the information she needed to, hopefully, find a sibling, she'd completely skimmed over the Armstrongs' family dynamics.

She needed to be more thorough, Ramona told herself sternly.

Cocking her head, she scrutinized the man in front

of her, doing her best to give off an aura of sweetness. She knew that she could be all but irresistible if she wanted to be. She eased her conscience by reminding herself that this was definitely not for personal gain. This was for her mother.

"Now that you mention it, you do look a little more robust and athletic than you—I mean, your brother—did yesterday." She was five-seven, not exactly a petite flower. But the man before her was taller, way taller. He looked even more so since she was sitting and he was not.

Ramona raised her eyes to his in a studied look of innocent supplication. A look she'd practiced more than once. "So he—your brother—can't hire me?"

Now she was getting it, Paul thought. "Not by himself, no."

Again she cocked her head, employing a certain come-hither look as she asked him, "Can he hire me if you hire me?"

Why did he feel as if the ground beneath his feet was turning from shale to sand, leaving him nothing solid to stand on? "Not without Lisa's okay," he heard himself say hoarsely.

Another country heard from, Ramona thought impatiently, trying to remember exactly how many Armstrongs worked at the institute. Her smile never wavered as she repeated, "Lisa?"

Paul nodded, trying not to stare. Was it his imagination, or did she somehow suddenly look more beautiful? "My younger sister. She's the head administrator here at the institute."

That had to have been the cold voice on the phone, Ramona thought. "Does anyone else have a vote?"

He smiled and she thought he had a rather nice smile. It softened his features and made him appear less distant and forbidding.

"No, that's it," he assured her. "Just the three of us."

She nodded slowly, as if taking it all in and digesting the information. What she was really doing was casting about for a way to appeal to him and make him let her remain.

"Well," she said slowly with a drop of seduction woven in, "we know that I have your brother's vote. Do I have yours?"

For one unguarded moment, he could have sworn that he felt some sort of a sharp pull, an attraction to this young woman. But then he told himself it was just that he had always appreciated beauty no matter where he came across it. He certainly couldn't allow it to cloud his judgment, especially when it came to the institute.

Still, a public relations manager might prove useful, he supposed. Paul was honest in his answer. "I'd have to think about it."

She appeared undaunted. "Well, that's better than 'no,'" Ramona allowed.

Faced with her optimism, Paul wavered a little more in his stand, shifting in a direction he knew that Lisa would easily disapprove. "I tell you what. Let me talk to the others and we'll get back to you."

Ramona smiled. It made him think of a sunrise. Warm and full of promise. And then she looked just a tad shy as she asked, "In the meantime, would it be all right if I drafted a press release?"

"A press release?" Paul echoed, confused. "About what?"

"About doctors Demetrios and Bonner joining your staff. Mr. Armstrong—Mr. *Derek* Armstrong," she amended, "said that so far, no mention had been made of the transition. I think it would be a big plus for the institute, not to mention that it would be a huge draw, as well." Not that the institute actually needed it, she thought. The rich and famous flocked here, and the masses followed. "These two researchers are very famous in their field."

"I know," he said, amused that she believed she was telling him something he wasn't aware of.

"Of course you do." Holding her breath just so allowed the right amount of pink to creep into her cheeks. She instinctively knew that Paul was the kind of man who reacted to blushes, even though it was as out of date as a silver disco ball. "I just meant that it should be brought to people's attention. It's positive re-inforcement." And then she flashed him another guile-less smile. "I promise I won't do anything with the draft until I get your—all of your," she amended, "okays."

She sounded so eager and upbeat, Paul found that

he hadn't the heart to tell her to wait until after he'd won Lisa over. Lisa could be difficult at times, especially if she felt that her territory was being encroached upon and threatened. Her earlier tirade was likely only the tip of the iceberg on this matter.

"That'll be fine," he told her and then he quickly walked out of the room before he wound up agreeing to something else.

He needed to find Derek and have a few choice words with his brother for putting him in this situation. A few *very* choice words.

He found Derek just outside his brother's office, engaged in what appeared to be a very private conversation with one of the newer and younger administrative assistants. From the looks of it, it appeared that groundwork for far more than further conversation was being laid.

Suppressing a sigh, Paul inserted himself between the exceedingly perky young redhead in the platform heels and his brother. "Excuse us, please, um—" He had no idea what the young woman's name was.

"Danielle." Both the young woman and Derek said the name at the same time, which caused them to exchange more covert looks. Paul heard the assistant smother a giggle.

"Danielle," Paul repeated with a slight nod of his head, "I need to speak with my brother."

"Of course." Inclining her head, the administrative

assistant drew away. But not before she exchanged one more overtly steamy, sexy glance with the institute's CFO.

Paul walked into his brother's recently remodeled office and waited for Derek to follow. Which Derek did. Languidly.

The moment the door was closed, Paul immediately started talking. "What the hell were you thinking, hiring that young girl?" he demanded.

Derek looked at him, apparently confused. "Who?"

"The one sitting in Connie Winston's old office. Your so-called PR manager."

If he was aware of the sarcasm in his brother's voice, Derek didn't show it. "Oh, you mean Ramona Tate." Derek grinned broadly, obviously pleased with himself. "That was a real lucky break."

Derek was usually more intuitive than this. Ordinarily, he picked up on tension. Maybe his brother thought it would all just go away if he didn't acknowledge it. *Think again, Derek.* If nothing else, Paul wanted some of the ground rules reaffirmed.

"Some of us," he told Derek, "don't think so."

Derek laughed shortly. "By 'some' I take it you mean Lisa and you." Even as he said the words amicably, he knew the answer. Just as he knew that their baby sister was behind this confrontation. Even as a kid, Lisa was into power plays. As the youngest of the Armstrong children, she always wanted to come out on top, to be the one the others listened to.

Putting his hand on Paul's shoulder, Derek said patiently, "Paul, you're an excellent physician and a wonderful chief of staff here at the institute. If you ask me, you deserve a lot more credit than you're getting. But let's be honest, there's no denying that the institute needs help."

"I got us help," Paul pointed out tersely. "I got Demetrios and Bonner to leave their hospital and join the institute. In case you missed it, they're the cutting-edge research team who—"

"I didn't miss it," Derek answered crisply, cutting in. "But I just might have been the only one around who didn't."

Paul had absolutely no idea what that even meant. "What?"

"Exactly," Derek declared as if Paul had made his point for him. "What newspaper was that where the press release announcing their joining the institute was run? Oh, wait, it wasn't," he said with exaggerated enlightenment. "Because we had no one manning our PR desk to make that press release. But we do now," he concluded with a smug, triumphant smile.

Paul was easygoing up to a point, but he dug in now. If he didn't take a stand here, he might as well just lie down and have Derek walk all over him. "Not until Lisa and I agree to hire her."

"Then agree," Derek told him, trying to control his irritation. "Because she's already hired."

"Not exactly."

"What do you mean 'not exactly'?" Derek wanted to know. "I hired her yesterday."

"And I put her on temporary notice."

The smile evaporated instantly. Derek exploded. "For God's sake, why?"

Paul dug deep for patience. Derek, he knew, was accustomed to doing whatever he wanted to unopposed. But when it came to the institute, important decisions had to involve all three of them. They'd agreed on that when they took over the famous facility from their ailing father.

As if it was the first time, Paul doled his words out evenly. "Because you can't just go off and do this kind of thing whenever you feel like it without at least consulting Lisa *and* me."

"So you're going to let Ramona go because you're mad at me?" he asked in abject disbelief. Derek shook his head in amazement. "Boy, leave it to you to be such a cliché."

Paul's gaze became flinty. "Excuse me?"

Derek frowned, exasperated. "That old chestnut about cutting off your nose to spite your face. That's what you're doing."

Any moment now, his brother was going to throw a tantrum, Paul thought. "You're carrying on as if I just fired Woodward and Bernstein. That girl looks like she's barely out of high school, let alone college. We implant embryos here, Derek, we don't hire them."

Derek raised his voice to be heard over him. "Ramona Tate is twenty-five years old and she has impressive credentials—"

"Which I'm sure you checked thoroughly." Paul couldn't help the note of sarcasm that came into his voice. He sincerely doubted that Derek had done anything but glance at her résumé.

Derek squared his shoulders indignantly. "I was getting to that."

Sure you were, Paul thought. "Want another old chestnut?"

Derek slanted a glance toward him, a suspicious look entering his eyes. "Like what?"

"Like you're putting the cart before the horse." In this case, he'd hired the woman and planned to rubber-stamp her references—if she even had any.

A deep chuckle escaped Derek's lips. "Maybe you didn't notice—and if you didn't, you'd be the only one who wouldn't—but this 'horse' has lines that could stop a charging rhino in his tracks."

Paul sighed, shaking his head. "So this is about your libido."

Derek rolled his eyes. "Unlike you, I have one, but in this case I was thinking of the institute."

Paul leaned a hip against his brother's desk. "This I have to hear."

"There's nothing wrong in having an extremely attractive—and able—woman to represent us. To be the 'face' of the Armstrong Fertility Institute." Seeing that he was losing Paul, Derek hurried to add, "Which would you rather look at when it comes to getting your information, a gnarled, short, bald, fat man or an attractive young woman who makes your blood surge and makes you think of fertility just by *looking* at her?"

"I'd just as soon get it in a report on my desk."

Derek threw up his hands. "You're hopeless, you know that?"

Paul made no comment on that. He didn't feel he needed to defend himself. This wasn't about him, *or* Derek. This was about their father's legacy. "How much is she costing the institute?"

Derek rallied for a second defense. "Not as much as you would think—and Ramona is worth every penny of it."

Paul gave his twin a knowing look. "I'll bet."

"Get your mind out of the gutter, Paul. I was referring to the press release I asked her to prepare."

Was that why the woman had asked him if she could draft a statement? "About?" he asked cautiously, wanting to see if the stories agreed.

"Your dynamic duo, of course. Bonner and Demetrios bring their own sterling reputations to the table—just as you planned." Derek wasn't above trying to butter his brother up if he had to. "We get the public focusing on that, they'll forget the rumors."

He blew out a breath, then looked at Paul hopefully. "So how about it, Paul? Can we take her off notice and just watch her work?" He put his arm around his brother's shoulders in a gesture of solidarity. "I promise you won't be sorry."

There was no way that Derek could guarantee that. "And if I am?"

Derek laughed. "Not even you can be that much of a stodgy old man." Derek tapped his brother's chest with the back of his hand. "Loosen up, Paul. You'll not only live longer, but you'll get to enjoy yourself, too."

"I *do* enjoy my life," Paul insisted. And he did. He was dedicated to continuing his father's work and to granting childless couples their fondest wish. That was more than enough for him.

Derek merely shook his head. "Can't see how, but okay. Do you know where Lisa is?"

Paul laughed quietly. "Most likely sharpening her tongue so she can give you a good lashing."

"That's why I want to head her off," Derek confessed. "I was hoping to make a preemptive strike."

Paul thought of the expression on Lisa's face when she burst into his office earlier. "Too late," he speculated.

Derek was not easily defeated. And he had the ability to talk someone to death—or at least until he got what he wanted.

"Maybe not," he countered as he went off in search of their sister. Ramona Tate was staying and that was that. He was *not* about to tolerate being overridden. The institute needed to continue to make money and that was not going to happen if people—wealthy people—stopped coming to avail themselves of what they had to offer here. Their focus needed to be redirected to a positive image, and Ramona Tate seemed just the person to do it.

Both he and the institute would benefit from that.

Chapter Three

Ramona already knew that there was nothing in this small office that could help her with her investigation. If there was data that could openly incriminate one or more of the staff at the institute for engaging in the wrongful substitution of eggs or sperm, it wouldn't be readily accessible. She was also fairly certain that nothing tangible would turn up to back the claim that too many embryos were being implanted purely to up the success ratio.

There was no way she was going to learn how to access records that had been archived just by sitting here, staring at the walls. Ramona wasn't even certain that there *were* archived records. Since they might prove to be incriminating, they might have been destroyed years ago. She knew for a fact that they weren't on any database within the institute.

All she could do was hope that Gerald Armstrong, who ran this facility until ill health had forced him into retirement, had been vain enough to hang on to everything—good or bad—that even remotely testified to his accomplishments and his genius. From what she'd read and heard, the man had a more than healthy ego.

If the senior Armstrong had played God and implanted her mother's eggs into someone, she thought, adrenaline rushing excitedly through her veins, that *had* to have been noted in the recipient's file. She might be looking for a needle in a haystack, but at least she'd know that there *was* a needle.

Dr. Gerald Armstrong had been in charge of operations and treatments when her mother had sold her eggs to the institute, Ramona thought. Pacing about her small office, she wondered now if there was any plausible excuse she could come up with in order to gain access to the man. All she needed was about ten minutes. She knew that these days he led a fairly low-key, quiet life, hardly ever leaving his home. He was cared for and looked after by his very long-suffering wife.

It had to be hell for both of them, Ramona thought. Emily Stanton Armstrong came from a good family and had a high social standing in the community when she married the up-and-coming pioneering doctor. The woman spent her days planning charitable events and her evenings attending them.

From her research, Ramona knew that the good doctor had made sure that he got his share of mileage out of the successes the institute achieved. Handsome, dynamic and blessed with the gift of gab, rumor had it that Gerald Armstrong had more than one illicit relationship. Mrs. Armstrong cast a blind eye to his dealings and partied harder.

Now they were almost like two shut-ins—he, more often than not, relegated to his wheelchair, she to nursing a man she had quite possibly learned to loathe.

Not exactly the type of people she wanted to have anything to do with, Ramona thought. Still, she was not above using any means, fair or foul, to achieve her main goal: finding out if her mother's desperate action had ultimately resulted in a child who could save her life.

For now, though, Ramona had no choice but to stay in her office and wait for Armstrong—be it Paul or Derek, or perhaps even Lisa—to come and tell her whether or not she was to stay on as PR manager.

Because she wasn't the type to waste time by aimlessly surfing the Web, Ramona decided to do exactly what she'd told Paul she was going to do: draft a press release about the research team who had recently been enticed to add their names to the fertility institute's roster.

Even though she was only twenty-five, she already had established several strong connections within the media world. Pulling a few strings, she was certain that she could get sufficient coverage for Demetrios and Bonner's shift from working at a teaching hospital to bringing their research program to the Armstrong Fertility Institute.

And as for the public, she'd already learned that they were mercurial, as fast to revere as to condemn. All it took were the right words in the right place to achieve either reaction. For the time being, it served her purpose to give the Armstrongs a little something to put in the plus column.

Her mouth curved as she thought about it. If everything went according to plan, this would amount to the calm before the storm. Because, if her information turned out to be correct, she intended to bring the Armstrong Fertility Institute down so fast, the pompous family would wind up choking on the dust that was kicked up.

She crossed back to the desk and sat down to work. Pausing just for a moment to find the right first word, her fingers soon flew across the keyboard, trying to keep up with her racing brain and coming in a close second.

Engrossed in wording the release so that it would pop as a whole, Ramona didn't hear the knock on her door. She also wasn't aware of that same door being opened a beat later.

Paul slipped in unobtrusively, a considerable feat for a man who measured six foot one. But then, he had the kind of quiet, easygoing manner that allowed him to blend in with the scenery at will. Unlike his outgoing brother, who had never been known to fade into the background, even for a moment, in his entire life. The very act would have been against everything that Derek stood for.

She looked diligent, Paul observed, completely involved in her work. She was obviously intent on doing a good job.

Maybe Derek had been right in hiring this young woman after all, he mused. Maybe a public-relations spokesperson was exactly what they needed to give them that much-needed shot in the arm. Good works didn't count for very much if no one knew you did them, and the public, fickle at best in their loyalties, couldn't exactly be expected to embrace something if they didn't know about it.

Paul took a step forward and cleared his throat.

The sound caught her attention and Ramona raised her eyes. The next moment she was clamping her lips together, stifling a gasp. When had Armstrong come in? "How long have you been standing there?"

A slight smile curved his mouth. "Long enough to discover that you nibble on your lower lip when you're thinking—or was that fretting?"

Fretting. Now, *there* was a word she hadn't heard in—well, maybe forever. This man definitely had stepped out of the last century. Quite possibly the first half of the last century, she speculated.

"No, no 'fretting,'" she answered with a straight face. "You were right the first time. I was just thinking something through. Don't worry. There's nothing in what I'm writing that should stir up any kind of concern." She gestured toward the screen, which, given its position, only she could see right now. "It's just the institute doctors' backgrounds, plus I've added a little family history for each of them."

Personal histories had never really interested him all that much. They were just fillers, padding that was easily eliminated. It was what a person did, not who their parents were, that mattered. Though he had to admit that maybe his own background tainted his view of things.

Still, he asked, "Do you think that's really necessary?"

As far as she was concerned, a person's history was the most interesting part. She always wanted to know what made people tick, how they got to be the way they were. She sincerely doubted that she was alone in this.

"People like to know who they're dealing with. It makes the whole challenging process of fertility treatment a little more down-to-earth for them—and a little less like science fiction."

Leaning back in what she hoped would continue to be her chair for at least a modest amount of time, Ramona did her best to appear relaxed. The very act belied the knots in her stomach. She laced her fingers before her and tried to sound cheerful as she asked, "So, what's the verdict?"

Technically, there was no official verdict yet. He told her what was happening. "I managed to send Derek to Lisa to apologize."

Well, that didn't sound very heartening. "For hiring me?" she asked. This would be the part where she would have gotten up and told him what he could do with his apology. But she wasn't being herself, she was being a subservient employee. She assumed that was what Paul Armstrong wanted and she was willing to go along with it, as long as it eventually got her access to the archives.

"For hiring you without consulting with the rest of us," Paul corrected.

That still didn't give her the answer she was hoping for. "So you're letting me go?" she guessed. She had trouble envisioning the woman who belonged to that cold voice over the phone giving her a thumbs-up. Even so, there was absolutely no way she was going to go without a fight. "Because if you are, Dr. Armstrong, you're going to regret it."

"Are you threatening me, Miss Tate?" he asked quietly.

"No, I'm telling you that you need me," she responded with feeling. "I'm very good at my job." Ramona straightened and squared her shoulders.

She made him think of a warrior princess. He had no idea where that had come from, only that it seemed like a very appropriate description.

"I'd like you to read what I've been writing before you have security eject me."

Paul held up his hand to stop her before her mouth launched into double time. The woman was already talking faster than he could listen. He had a feeling that, like Derek, Ramona Tate could talk with the best of them, easily winning battles simply by wearing her opposition down.

"No one's ejecting you, Miss Tate," he assured her. "You have a temporary stay of execution."

The surprise came and went from her face in an instant. Had he blinked, Paul suspected he wouldn't have seen it at all.

"How temporary?" she wanted to know, banking down her eagerness.

"That remains to be seen," he told her. It depended on whether she actually got results that would do them any good. For now, he was willing to give her the benefit of the doubt. "Why don't we just take this one step at a time, shall we?"

"That's all I ever wanted, an opportunity to prove myself to you—whichever 'you' I happen to be talking to," she added with an amused smile. Rising, she cocked her head just a tad as she peered at him closely, her eyes swiftly taking inventory and reviewing everything she noted. And then she made her decision. "You're Dr. Paul," she declared with just a hint of triumph.

He hid his amusement. "What makes you so certain?" he asked.

Even though he felt that there was a world of difference between his brother and him, Paul knew that as far as looks went, he and Derek were close to interchangeable unless they were standing beside one another. It was only then that someone might notice that Derek was thinner, while he looked as if he availed himself of the gym's facilities whenever he could, which he did.

When they were younger, both of their parents managed to confuse one with the other, in part, Paul suspected, because neither parent ever really took the time to get to know either of them. Although, if he thought about it, Paul had a feeling that if his parents *had* taken the time, it would only have been Derek who would have garnered their focused attention.

It wasn't only the squeaky wheel that got greased, it was the noisy, silver-tongued brother who ultimately got all the attention.

Ramona smiled up at him. The smile penetrated clear down to his bones. "Your eyes."

He waited, but she didn't elaborate. "What about my eyes?" he pressed. He fully expected her to say something to the effect that they were dull, that Derek was the one whose eyes looked as if they held a host of secrets and the promise of excitement.

But she surprised him. "You're the one with the kind eyes," Ramona said. "Your brother's eyes are…unfathomable."

Maybe she didn't have such a happy way with words after all. Paul interpreted her meaning. "So Derek is the man of mystery while I'm the flat, two-dimensional one."

Her perfectly shaped eyebrows drew together into

a V. She looked surprised at his interpretation of her assessment.

"Not at all," she protested. "On an absolute level, you'd be the one who people would trust, Dr. Armstrong, not your brother. They'd go to him looking for a good time, not honesty."

Ramona firmly believed that it was never too early to begin laying groundwork in order to build a viable relationship. That was her goal at the moment to build a connection with Paul. She could accomplish more at a quicker pace if she had one of the Armstrongs in her corner, and Paul, although reserved, struck her as the one who was more real, more open. She had the feeling that Derek had his own, private agenda, one he meant to pursue no matter what. A man like that couldn't be manipulated.

Besides, Derek Armstrong was far too into himself to be of any use to her.

Paul shook his head ever so slightly. "I already said you had a temporary stay of execution, Miss Tate. There's no need to try to flatter me."

Annoyed with herself that she'd come across so transparent, nonetheless Ramona managed to rally quickly. "I wasn't flattering, I was telling it the way I saw it," she informed him simply.

She might have given him a simple answer, Paul mused, but he had the impression that this woman was anything but that. As a matter of fact, he would have been willing to say that, despite declarations of honesty and truth, there was something Ramona Tate was keeping back.

The fleeting thought intrigued him.

In case she believed he was fishing for more validation, he changed the subject. "By the way, about your references—"

Ramona was one jump ahead of him. She'd learned that a good defense was to have a good offense. "I have them right here." Reaching for her oversize purse, she pulled it toward her, then flipped the locks open. "Your brother said he'd be getting around to reviewing them eventually, but I think they should be a matter of record, don't you?" Taking out a light blue file that contained more than a few letters of praise, she offered the folder to him. "There's also a copy of my academic transcript and employment history," she told him.

Taking the folder, Paul opened it and scanned a few of the pages. There were letters from college professors and from news editors, some of whom had the logos of local TV stations stamped on them. One was from the *Washington Post*. He'd expected one letter, perhaps two. If asked, he would have said that she was too young for more than that.

"And you said that you were just twenty-five?" he asked incredulously.

Maybe Monty had laid it on a little thick, Ramona thought. Monty Durham was the computer geek/wizard she'd befriended in her first year in college. He'd been so grateful to have someone to talk to, he became

Sancho Panza to her female Don Quixote. There wasn't anything that Monty couldn't make a computer do, including spew out lies and make them look like gospel. There also wasn't anything that Monty wouldn't do for her.

"I graduated two years early," she told Paul by way of an explanation.

Which was true. Eager to start leaving her mark in the world, Ramona had opted for an accelerated course of study. It had allowed her to crunch four years of high school into three and then do the same with college. To make it work, she'd attended school year-round, picking up courses part-time in the summer. In her spare time, she had also worked any job in her field she could get her hands on. That in turn gave her a much-needed solid core for her résumé. Monty had done the rest, embellishing where he could. He was also responsible for half the letters of recommendation in the folder.

She was unusual, Paul decided, he'd give her that. "In my experience, most people like to extend their college experience if they can."

"Maybe so," she allowed. "But I wanted to get started with my life," she countered. "College was great," she added quickly, not wanting him to think she was bucking for some kind of sainthood, "but college isn't life. It's more like the TV version." Angling the monitor so that it turned in his direction, Ramona realized that she'd come full circle and made the offer again. "Would you like to read what I've written so far?"

That would probably be the best way to determine whether or not she could actually do them some good, he thought. Or if having her around was just Derek's way of having eye candy on hand.

"Actually, I would."

Smiling, she hit the key combination that caused the wireless printer in the corner to come to life. Within moments, it produced the four pages she'd composed. Ramona crossed to the machine and removed the sheets, then returned and handed them to Paul.

And that was when he realized that he'd gotten caught up in watching her move, and Paul found that for once he couldn't fault his brother for admiring Ramona's looks. He had to admit, the sway of her hips was something to behold. It was enough to even make a man believe in Santa Claus.

Chapter Four

Back in his office, Paul read through Ramona's pages.

Even if he wanted to, Paul could find no fault with the rough draft that she had given him to review. Obviously the new public relations manager definitely had a way with words.

Maybe, Paul thought, putting the four sheets of paper down on his desk, Derek was actually onto something.

There was a quick rap on his office door and before he could say, "Come in," the person on the other side of the knock did.

Speak of the devil.

Derek stuck his head in, holding on to the doorknob as if he was prepared to make a quick getaway. Paul couldn't help wondering if something was wrong. Derek seemed edgier to him these days. Was that just because of the tense climate at the institute, or was there more to it than that?

"You can stop holding your breath," Derek informed him cheerfully.

"I wasn't aware that I was." Paul waited for his brother to follow up with an explanation.

"Sure you were. About Little Miss PR's fate," Derek prompted when Paul continued to look at him quizzically. "I got Lisa to come on board with our decision."

"'Our' decision?" Paul asked, emphasizing the plural possessive. Was Derek trying to share the blame, or the glory?

"Sure." Derek looked surprised that he was even questioning that it was a joint effort. "You wanted to hire her, too, didn't you?"

"Well, yes, now," Paul admitted, because he had been won over, but he certainly hadn't started out that way. "However—"

Derek breezed right past his brother's "however" as he continued his narrative. "I convinced Lisa that we need a professional to help take the tarnish off the institute's reputation. Ramona stays."

Paul thought how angry Lisa had looked when she'd stormed into his office earlier. He shook his head in wonder. "Derek, you could probably sweet-talk the devil into giving you back your soul, couldn't you?"

Derek inclined his head. He saw no reason to argue. "If I had to." And then he grinned. The harried look he'd sported earlier faded as he asked, "By the way, you wouldn't be referring to our youngest sister as the devil, would you?"

Paul blanched. That was all he needed, to have Lisa think he was calling her names behind her back. "No, I would *never*—"

Derek laughed, waving away the rest of whatever his twin was about to protest. "Take it easy, Paul, I was only kidding. You're so nonconfrontational you wouldn't even call the devil a devil."

Paul read between the lines. "Are you telling me I'm spineless?"

Derek sobered for a second. His voice was devoid of any cynicism or sarcasm. For a fleeting moment, it almost seemed to be a tad wistful. "No, I'm telling you that everyone thinks of you as the 'good' brother. The nice guy."

There was something in his brother's voice, an unfathomable undercurrent that caught Paul's attention. This was the second time today that he felt as if a member of his family was hiding something, keeping something back. Prodding, he had a feeling, was going to be as futile with Derek as it had been with Olivia, but he wouldn't have been Paul if he didn't try.

"Is something on your mind, Derek?"

And just like that, the serious look in Derek's eyes

completely vanished. The cocky, confident air was back. In spades.

"Something's *always* on my mind, Paul." He winked broadly. "It's called responsibilities. Gotta fly. I'm heading out."

Paul tried to pin Derek down to something specific. "For the day?"

"For the rest of the week." That, Paul knew, was what he was afraid of. Of late, Derek behaved more like a hurricane, striking swiftly and then moving on just as quickly. "Maybe longer," Derek was saying. "Listen, I was going to help familiarize Ramona with the institute, give her a tour of the place, answer any questions she might have, that kind of thing. But now that I'm not going to be here, I'd really appreciate if you did the honors for me."

"Why aren't you going to be here?" Paul wanted to know. For his part, he was *always* here. Or at least it felt that way. He was not only chief of staff at the institute, but he saw his patients here, as well. Derek, on the other hand, hardly seemed to be present at all.

"Something came up" was all that Derek would say. "I need you to fill in for me. Will you do it?" To the untrained ear, it sounded as if Derek was giving him a choice.

But Paul knew better.

He frowned. He wasn't good with people in any prolonged capacity. And he was exceedingly bad when it came to making small talk. Despite their age difference—he was thirty-six to her twenty-five—he had a feeling that Ramona Tate was far more of a sophisticated creature than he was. This was out of his ballpark.

"Can't Lisa do it?"

Derek laughed shortly, dismissing the suggestion, or, in this case, request. "Lisa's got a lot on her plate right now, too. Besides, she'd be too busy sizing Ramona up to be of any help. You know how competitive our baby sister can get."

This was true, but she'd always been fiercely competitive with her three siblings—not, to his knowledge, with strangers.

"Why would she be competitive?"

Derek sighed, shaking his head. "She's female. In case you haven't noticed, brother dear, so is Ramona."

That was just the trouble. He *had* noticed. Really noticed. Ramona Tate was a stunning young woman. Just the type he could envision Derek—or their father, in his day—pursuing.

Without saying he would do it, he pressed Derek for some kind of specifics. "Where did you say you were going again?"

"I didn't."

And with that noncommunicative response, Derek closed the door and, for all intents and purposes, the institute's CFO vanished.

Paul sighed. That was so typical. There were times when Derek treated the institute as his own personal playground, someplace to pop in, stay just long enough to stir things up, then hop a plane and go back to New York, where he actually lived.

If that was even where he was going this time. Derek was a fine one to bandy the word *responsibilities* about. For the past few months, he'd certainly been shirking his while stepping on everyone else's toes, egging them on to pick up the slack he'd created.

Paul glanced down at the paper he'd just finished reading, his mind shifting to the problem Derek had left in his wake. He didn't have time for the so-called orientation tour that Derek had palmed off on him—at least not today. But he could tell the woman that she had her job and that, by the way, she'd done a rather nice one on the press release she'd just worked up.

Paul had never cared for empty flattery, but he did believe in telling someone if they'd done good work. It was something he'd learned not to take for granted. Praise was something that he'd never heard himself when he was growing up. His father hadn't been reticent when it came to acknowledgment, he just wasn't around all that much to begin with. It was hard to honestly comment on any accomplishments if you didn't know about them; if you hadn't been around to see or hear anything about them. Dr. Gerald Armstrong always seemed either to be *at* the institute he'd founded, or *on his way* to the institute.

Paul swore to himself that if he ever had any children of his own—something he was doubtful at this point would ever come about—he would never miss an opportunity to praise them if they did something well.

Hell, he'd even praise them for an *attempt* to do something well. People needed to be encouraged, especially children. That was why he'd initially become a doctor. To get the great Gerald Armstrong's approval. To get Gerald Armstrong's attention, at least for five minutes.

Neither really happened, but somewhere along the line, he grew to love his work. He supposed that made him one of the lucky ones after all.

Paul was just about to go see Ramona and discuss her release when there was another knock on his door. Had Derek changed his mind and decided to stay? He figured it was probably too much to hope for.

"Come in."

And he was right. It was too much to hope for. It wasn't Derek who walked into his office. It was Olivia.

"I saw your wunderkind doctor," she told him. There was no sarcasm in her voice. The title was bestowed in earnest.

Paul noticed that her face was flushed. Was that a good sign? Or a bad one?

"And?" Paul asked when she didn't continue. He gestured for her to take a chair.

She did, perching her weight on the edge of the cushion as if she anticipated the need to fly away at any moment.

"And he said there was a chance I could become

pregnant. Slim, but a chance," she added breathlessly, clinging to the word *chance* as if it were a lifeline.

Paul nodded. He more than anyone knew how iffy that statement was. But he was not about to rain on Olivia's parade.

"Well, he would be the one to know. There's none better," he assured her. For a moment, he sat there just looking at Olivia, debating whether or not to back away. He decided to try one more time to get her to open up. "Livy, is it Jamison?" he asked, referring to his brother-in-law, the up-and-coming junior senator from Massachusetts and media darling.

Olivia looked up sharply, a porcelain doll about to shatter. Her eyes were wary. "Is what Jamison?"

Paul had no idea how to phrase this, he just knew he had to get it out into the open somehow. He couldn't shake the feeling that there was more to his sister's unhappiness than just the failure to become pregnant.

"Is Jamison pressing you to become pregnant?" He knew how important lineage and legacy were to the Mallorys. They were practically their own dynasty, the young lions of the world, determined to leave their mark. Part of that involved offspring. "I mean, there are other ways to go, you know. You could adopt, or have a surrogate mother who—"

Olivia began shaking her head the moment he'd said that there were other ways to go. She didn't want to hear it.

"No. I want to *feel* this, to do this myself." Olivia

pressed her hand against her flat belly, splaying her fingers out beneath her chest.

Paul looked into her eyes for a long moment. "Having a baby doesn't solve anything, you know," he told her quietly. "It usually creates its own set of unique problems."

"I know that." There was tension wrapped around each word and he noticed that Olivia was clasping and unclasping her hands in her lap.

Paul pressed again, more succinctly now. "Are you sure everything is all right between you and Jamison?"

"Yes," she finally snapped. "Which is more than I can say about between you and me if you keep asking these ridiculous questions."

This wasn't getting him anywhere. Paul retreated. "Sorry. I'm just concerned about you, Olivia, that's all."

She pressed her lips together and took in a deep breath in an attempt to calm herself. "I appreciate that and I'm sorry, too. I really didn't mean to snap at you like that, it's just that it seems like everywhere I look these days, I see women either pushing a baby carriage or being pregnant and looking as if they're about to pop at any second. Everybody is pregnant but me." Her voice quavered and she looked down at her knotted fingers. "We've been trying for five years now. Five *long* years."

"Yes, I know. You told me," he replied gently.

Olivia abruptly rose to her feet, a deer about to flee. Paul rounded his desk, coming to her side. Though he wasn't a demonstrative person by nature, seeing his sister like this tugged on his heartstrings. He hugged her, albeit awkwardly.

"Everything's going to be all right, Livy," he promised.

"I hope so," she murmured against his shoulder. "I sincerely hope so."

There was yet another knock on his door. Undoubtedly that was his nurse, here to remind him that he had patients to see this afternoon. Anxious patients who felt exactly like his sister.

"Come in," he called out.

Ramona came in just as he gave his sister another bracing hug before releasing her.

Olivia stepped back.

Surprised, certain that she'd inadvertently walked in on something, Ramona instantly looked down at the rug as if it had suddenly become fascinating. "Oh, I'm sorry. I didn't mean to interrupt anything."

"You didn't," Paul told her crisply. "This is my sister Olivia Armstrong Mallory."

Ramona looked at the other woman, a wariness automatically entering her eyes. Another Armstrong. Another hurdle?

"Someone else who has to approve my being hired?" she asked politely.

Turning from the woman in the doorway, Olivia looked at him quizzically.

"Long story," Paul told her, forestalling any questions on her part. "And I have to be somewhere."

Olivia slipped the strap of her designer purse onto her shoulder. "So do I," she told him. "Thanks for getting me in to see Dr. Demetrios," she said, then nodded at Ramona before slipping out. "Nice meeting you."

But you didn't, Ramona thought. The fourth branch on the Armstrong family tree—this had to be Senator Mallory's wife, she realized—hadn't learned her name, making the introduction incomplete.

"She didn't," Ramona said out loud to Paul once the door was closed again.

That had come out of nowhere. Much like the woman herself, he observed now. "She didn't what?"

"Meet me," Ramona told him. Because Paul looked at her as if she'd just lapsed into a foreign dialect, she elaborated, "You gave me her name, but you didn't give her mine."

She was right. Paul lifted one shoulder in a careless shrug.

"She was in a hurry," he explained, then glanced at his watch. "And so am I."

"Then I won't keep you," Ramona promised, getting down to business. She subtly stepped into his path so that he couldn't leave his office without answering her. "I just wanted to know if you have any changes you want me to incorporate into the article."

His mind still on his sister's troubled demeanor, he looked at Ramona blankly. "Article?"

"The press release," she prompted. Seeing the pages on his desk, she pointed to them for emphasis. "That."

"Oh." What was it about this woman that seemed to drive any coherent thoughts out of his head? Paul glanced back at his desk, as if seeing the pages there would crystallize his thoughts. "No, no changes. It's very good just the way it is."

She knew she should let it go at that. But she couldn't. It wasn't vanity that prodded her, just a desire to make sure that everything was clear and aboveboard.

"Then you really did read it?" Her eyes held his. She liked to think that she could tell if a person was lying.

"Every last word," Paul assured her. And then he added, "You have a very fortuitous way with words, Ramona." There was genuine admiration in his voice. "I know learned colleagues who sweat bullets just to get out a paragraph. You whipped that whole thing out in what, twenty minutes?"

"Ten," Ramona corrected. "I spent the other ten praying."

Whatever he might have expected her to say, that didn't even come close. Maybe he'd misheard her. "Praying?"

Ramona nodded. He watched her hoop earrings swing in time to the rhythm she'd created. "That you'd come back and tell me that you've all agreed to let me stay on." She put on the most earnest face she could. "I really want this job."

It seemed odd to him that anyone would get so caught up or passionate about a public-relations position. "Why?"

Mentally, Ramona crossed her fingers. She really did hate lying, even though it did come with the territory. Right now, she needed to be convincing. Ultimately, in order to do what she had to, she wanted Paul Armstrong to think of her as an ally. The sooner she gained the man's trust, the easier it would be to gain access to other records.

"Because as far as I'm concerned, the work that's being done here at the institute is of paramount importance."

Even though he was still in a hurry, her words made him pause. Crossing his arms before him, he took a moment to study his newest staff member. "So this is a crusade for you?"

Ramona's already dazzling smile grew brighter. "In a manner of speaking, yes."

He wanted to believe her. Things would be a great deal simpler if he just could and let it go at that. Maybe the betrayal of their former employee had put him on his guard, making him more suspicious than he ordinarily was. Or maybe he was just being supersensitive, but for the third time today, he felt he was in the presence of someone who wasn't being completely up-front with him. Someone who, for whatever reason, was holding something back.

Although, he had to admit that when it came to Ramona Tate, he hadn't a clue what that "something" might be. He didn't know the woman well enough for that. It was just a hunch. A feeling.

He was being far too paranoid, he upbraided himself. There was no real reason not to believe that the young woman was being honest with him. After all, he was the one who'd posed the question, who'd prodded her. It was possible that Ramona was every bit as altruistic as she presented herself to be.

Possible, he reasoned, but was it actually probable? He really wasn't all that sure that the answer to that was yes. However, only time would tell.

Chapter Five

He should be on his way, Paul thought and yet, here he was, still lingering. Still sharing space with this woman with the expressive eyes.

"Derek asked me to take you on a tour of the institute and to give you a miniorientation," he told her.

Her natural curiosity kicked in. "Why doesn't he give me the tour himself?"

Paul took the question to mean that she would have preferred his brother's company to his. He understood that. People always gravitated to Derek. He was the outgoing one, the one with the ability to make people laugh. The one who could defuse any situation and had a story to fit every occasion.

Ordinarily, it didn't bother him to have someone prefer Derek over him. He was used to it. Why it bothered him this time was something he wasn't about to let himself explore.

"He had to leave," Paul told her.

She nodded, accepting the excuse at face value. "So, when do you want to get started? Now's fine with me," she volunteered.

She certainly did seem eager. "Unfortunately, I don't have time today. I have several patients scheduled for this afternoon."

Her eyes widened ever so slightly and he found himself being drawn in. "So you practice medicine as well as oversee the staff here."

"Yes, why does that surprise you?" he wanted to know.

She laughed, adding a touch of self-consciousness to the sound, as if she hadn't expected to be caught. She knew how to play her role well. "I didn't take you for a multitasker."

He knew he should have already been on his way to his other office. His sense of responsibility had him making a point of being early rather than just on time, but her reply caused more questions to pop up. He didn't think of himself as the kind of person that people formed any sort of impression about—unless they felt they had to or when being in contact with him directly affected their lives.

"All right, I'll bite. What *did* you take me for?" he asked.

There was no hesitation. Ramona had the answer all worked out. "Someone who is very focused. Who follows the rules. Someone who does one thing at a time and who does that one thing very, very well."

He realized he was watching her lips as she spoke and he looked away. "Sorry to disappoint you."

"You didn't," she assured him quickly. "Actually, I don't mind being wrong when it turns out to be a pleasant surprise." She said it with such feeling, he half expected her next words to be "gotcha."

But they weren't.

Realizing that she was waiting for him to say something further, he finally asked, "How's tomorrow for you?"

Ramona smiled before answering. As hackneyed as it might have sounded to someone had he voiced his sentiments out loud, her smile really *did* seem to fill the room with sunshine. Maybe he needed to get out more, Paul thought.

"Tomorrow's fine. What time?"

"Early," he told her. "I have a procedure scheduled for ten o'clock, so why don't we get together about eight—unless that's too early for you."

"No, it can even be earlier if you'd prefer. I'm a morning person," she volunteered cheerfully.

"Eight will be early enough," he assured her, all but riveted by her smile.

It took effort to look away and even more effort to

get himself to walk out of the office and put distance between them.

The problem was Ramona had started to walk out at the same moment that he did. They found themselves together in the doorway; their bodies wound up brushing up against one another. A host of shock waves seemed to travel right through Paul, and he pulled back instantly as if propelled by a live wire.

"I'm so sorry," he apologized quickly, hoping that she didn't think he'd done that on purpose. Had he been Derek, he realized, he probably would have—and then smoothed it over with his golden tongue.

Something else they didn't have in common.

Incredibly, her smile seemed to widen even more and there was a hint of laughter in her eyes as she absolved him of all blame.

"That's all right," she assured him as if she realized it had been an accident on his part. "And for the record, I don't bite."

Even though he opened his mouth to respond, Paul had no comeback for that. His mind had gone completely blank in the face of her smile. He was really going to have to work on that, he chided himself

Mumbling "Tomorrow," Paul hurried down the hall to his other office, grateful that he could retreat somewhere.

Ramona stood in his doorway for a moment longer, watching the quietest member of the Armstrong tribunal disappear down the corridor. She wasn't really sure what to make of Dr. Paul Armstrong. If she didn't know any better, she would have said that the man seemed almost sweet. But that wasn't possible, not given the overall circumstances.

One thing she did know was that Dr. Paul Armstrong was going to be the subject of some heavy Internet research tonight.

Time was that after she'd put in a full day's work, she'd head for her cozy little apartment, eager to enjoy a little well-deserved solitude. Dinner most likely would be something she'd have delivered. She'd wind up consuming it while sitting on her chocolate-colored sofa—purchased expressly to hide a multitude of sins, otherwise known as indelible stains—and channel surfing. It was her way of unwinding.

But these days, her own gratification, not to mention rest, was usually postponed, if not put on hold altogether. Instead, she would wind up swinging by the house where she had grown up. The house where her mother still lived.

The key phrase here, Ramona thought, changing lanes to pass a slow-moving SUV, being "still lived."

Ramona became aware that her grip on the steering wheel had tightened and she forced herself to loosen it—while still keeping a grip on her fragile emotions.

Once upon a time, not all that long ago, she'd been so eager to make her own way, find her own path in the world. But even as she did, she was very aware of the solid foundation she had in her life. Aware that if ever anything went wrong, or she needed a haven, she had her mother, someone who would always be there for her. *Always.* And if everything was falling apart around her, her mother could always make her feel that it was going to be all right.

Until now.

The threat of mortality, of death always hovering in the background, an invisible wraith that had the power to steal absolutely *everything* from her, was now ever present.

Ramona knew it was childish, but even so, on some level she felt that she could stave off the threat of her mother's demise for another day if she just swung by the house and saw her for a little while in the evening. Some nights, "a little while" stretched out into the wee hours of the morning. At other times, she didn't bother going home at all, crashing in her old room instead.

Turning onto her mother's street, Ramona was aware that she was once again holding her breath, the way she did now every time she came. She only released it after a swift scan of the surrounding area told her that there was no ambulance parked nearby, no paramedics rushing in or out of the New England–style house that, according to family legend, her mother had fallen in love with thirty-five years ago.

All clear, Ramona thought, pulling up onto the recently repaved driveway.

Taking a moment to collect her things—her purse and the state-of-the-art laptop that went just about everywhere with her—Ramona got out and locked her vehicle, then made her way to the front door.

She paused, juggling purse and briefcase, searching for the keys that habit always had her dropping into her purse the moment she took them out of the ignition. She knew she should just hold the keys in her hand, but that never seemed to happen. She always wound up playing a frustrating game of hide-and-seek in front of the door before locating her keys.

This time, Ramona didn't have to. The front door opened before she could pull her keys out of her purse again.

Katherine Tate, or what was left of her these days, stood in the doorway, one hand on the doorjamb to support herself. There was a slight smile on her lips as she looked at her daughter fondly.

"I thought I heard your car pull up." A tiny "yip" had her mother amending her words. "Actually, Roxy was the one who heard you pull up," she confessed, referring to the tiny, energized mix-breed puppy that was all but tap-dancing behind her, trying to get at Ramona. "How she can tell your car apart from all the others that pass by, I have absolutely no idea. But she's never wrong." Placing her very thin hand on her daughter's shoulder to anchor herself, the five-foot-two woman stood up on her toes in order to press a kiss on Ramona's cheek. "How's my famous undercover daughter doing?"

Shifting her briefcase to the same side as her purse,

Ramona linked her free arm through her mother's as if they were just two carefree girlfriends, walking and chatting, instead of a daughter who was attempting to unobtrusively guide her mother back inside the house.

"That's a contradiction in terms, Mom. If I was famous, I couldn't get away with being undercover. I'd be recognized immediately." With a wink she pointed out, "I'd rather be good than famous."

"To me you're both," Katherine declared with great feeling.

Ramona beamed at her mother, biting back a wave of fear. Life couldn't go on if anything happened to her mother, she thought.

Hear that, God? You can't have her. I need her too much.

"I can always count on you to pick up my spirits," Ramona said to her mother. Roxy eagerly scurried back and forth. It was the dog's way of showing she was happy to see her.

"Why?" Katherine asked, slipping her arm out and shutting the door behind them as they walked in. She flipped the lock into place then slowly turned around to face her again. "Do your spirits need picking up?"

They did, but only because seeing her mother like this, a shell of her former vibrant, youthful self, was always a shock to her system for the first few minutes. She didn't know why she expected her to look exactly the way she had a little over six months ago. Probably because she still liked to believe in miracles and secretly prayed that one would occur in the hours that she was away from the house and her mother.

But the miracle just didn't happen.

It will. As soon as I find who your eggs went to, Mom, it will, she silently promised.

"Just a tough day," she said, knowing Katherine expected some kind of response. Ramona attributed her own success as an investigative reporter as something that came naturally to her thanks to her mother, who would approach a subject from an endless multitude of angles until she got what she was after. Surrendering or giving up were never considered options.

Ramona was aware that her mother's breathing was becoming labored. It took very few steps to tire her out these days. Katherine sank down on the sofa in the living room. Roxy instantly hopped onto the seat beside her mistress. Smiling wearily at the dog, she stroked it as she looked at her and asked, "Where is it again that you're pretending to work?"

"I'm not pretending, Mom," Ramona corrected fondly. She thought of the article she'd written for the press release. It was damn good. Even Derek Armstrong's stone-faced evil twin had liked it. "I really *am* working."

"But you're also digging, aren't you?" The question was merely for form's sake. Katherine knew the kind of work her daughter actually did. She was exceedingly proud of the path that Ramona had chosen.

"Yes, I am," Ramona answered.

Except that no real "digging" had taken place yet. She needed to get to know people a little better before she could safely start asking questions without arousing suspicion. She had, she felt, a perfect cover in her role as public-relations manager, and the tour that Paul Armstrong had promised her was going to be an immense help in getting her started.

"So what is this place where you're working undercover?" And then, before her daughter could answer, Katherine's eyes narrowed. "It's not one of these so-called escort places, is it? Because I saw an exposé on one of those magazine programs the other night and I really don't want you associating with people like that."

Ramona suppressed a smile. Her mother still felt she could shelter her from the world's darker elements. In a way, she almost found it sweet. There was no way she could have ever reached her present position not having dealt, at least fleetingly, with the seamier side of life. But she'd never want her mother to worry and was rather relieved that she could set her mind at ease without having to lie.

"No, it's not a 'so-called escort place,'" Ramona assured her. "And honestly, Mom, the less you know about it right now, the better."

It wasn't exactly the truth. She just didn't want to raise her mother's hopes by telling her that she was trying to track down a possible sibling. If she told her that she was working at the Armstrong Fertility Institute, her mother would make the obvious connection: that she was there to get access to the archives and to locate the couple who had profited by her desperate donation. If there were no siblings to be found, her own disappointment would be difficult enough to deal with. Maintaining a positive attitude was exceedingly important right now.

Katherine drew her own conclusions from what her daughter *wasn't* saying. Her concern was palatable. "Then it *is* dangerous."

"No, it's not dangerous, Mom," Ramona was quick to tell her with feeling. "It's that if you don't know, you won't accidentally let something slip when you're talking to one of the checkers at the supermarket or the beauty salon. Or one of your friends. Undercover means just that—undercover. Secret," she added, though she knew it was overkill.

Katherine looked just the slightest bit hurt. "When have I ever betrayed a confidence?"

"I wasn't thinking of betrayal, Mom. I was thinking of being human and last time I checked—" Ramona patted the hand that wasn't stroking Roxy "—you were most definitely human."

Her mother sighed quietly. "At least for a little while longer. Then I'll be a guardian angel, watching over you."

Ramona completely dismissed the serious part of Katherine's statement, refusing to give it any credence by even insisting that her mom had more than a little time left. She defused the moment the way she always did, with humor. "I don't think God lets you pick out your own assignments."

"Why not?" Katherine wanted to know. "It's heaven, isn't it?"

Ramona didn't bother suppressing her grin. "And your idea of heaven is watching over me?"

"Yes," Katherine answered with feeling. It drained her meager supply of energy for a moment.

Ramona laughed and shook her head. "Oh, Mom, we've got to get you out more."

"That would be lovely," Katherine agreed wistfully. "The minute I'm better—if I get better," she qualified, "you and I will do the town."

"The minute you're better—and you *will* be," Ramona emphasized fiercely, "I'm going to get you a guy and the *two of you* are going to do the town. You can do the town with me anytime."

Katherine rolled her eyes. Roxy, having lain down and been stroked into sleep, was snoring gently. "Oh, Ramona, why would I need a guy?"

Ramona grinned as she leaned over and patted her mother's hand again. "It'll come back to you, Mom. If not, I have a book I can lend you."

Katherine laughed and Ramona paused to listen to the soft, melodic sound, thinking how very much she loved hearing her mother laugh.

She intended to move heaven and earth if she had to, in order to continue hearing that sound for the next half century or so.

* * *

It was late.

Very late.

Paul had already put in a full day and then some as far as he was concerned. He was actually on his way out of the institute when his pager had gone off.

A quick call to his answering service told him that the McGees were frantically on their way in. Allison McGee was spotting and they were terrified that she was going to lose the babies she was carrying. The woman at the answering service said that Marc McGee sounded as if he was the on verge of having a heart attack and was barely coherent. He was driving and shouting into his cell phone at the same time.

Paul knew that he could have easily turned their case over to one of the more than competent doctors on the staff, but he knew that seeing him would calm Allison down a little.

And besides, he felt a personal obligation to the couple, just as he felt a personal obligation to every couple he counseled and worked with.

So he called Marc and told the frantic father-to-be that he would meet them at the nearby hospital where he had surgical privileges. The McGees arrived in the parking lot, tires screeching, less than five minutes later. Knowing what part of town they were coming from, he judged that they'd have to have done eighty all the way. Paul and an attendant greeted them with a wheelchair and Paul personally helped Allison out of the vehicle and into the chair.

What he'd hoped was just an aberration had turned into a premature delivery. A rather difficult one at that, requiring the services of two other obstetricians besides himself. But at the end of the ordeal, Allison and Marc had two viable sons, both now sleeping peacefully in their incubators. They were alive and that was the only thing that mattered.

And he was beat beyond measure. If he tried to drive home now, he had a feeling that he would undoubtedly be the subject of headlines tomorrow: Head of Staff of Armstrong Fertility Institute Caught Driving Erratically and Arrested. Drug or Alcohol Abuse Suspected. Possibly Both.

Or at least something along those lines. The press loved building you up and then tearing you down and the institute, for the moment, was in the tear-down stage. Since he had absolutely no desire to fall asleep behind the wheel, he decided that he would be better off sacking out on the couch in his office for at least an hour until he got his energy back.

With a weary sigh, he lay down on the leather sofa. He was asleep within five seconds.

Chapter Six

Paul felt the beads of sweat forming along his forehead. His hair stuck to his forehead. His limbs felt too heavy to lift. He had no more control over any part of his body.

He was having that dream again.

The one where he was trying to find his way to his office and the more he walked toward it, the farther away the office became.

Frustration and anxiety filled him. His breathing grew more shallow. His lungs began to ache. He kept walking, going faster now.

The corridor shifted. Instead of going straight, it became a series of twists and turns that led him down unfamiliar hallways. And all the while his sense of urgency continued building. Building until it grew to almost unbearable proportions.

Just as he thought he finally saw his office at the end of the long, tunnel-like hallway, the ground beneath his feet disappeared and he found himself plummeting into a ravine.

The churning waters below threatened to drown him and then carelessly wash his body away, casting it wantonly where no one would ever find him.

Then suddenly, unlike all the other times he'd had this unnerving dream, there was someone touching his arm.

Someone grabbing it and shaking him.

Someone was saving him, keeping him from being swept out to sea. He was saved!

More frustration assaulted him because he couldn't make out the face of the person who had rescued him at the very last, possible moment.

And then he heard the voice—a woman who had hold of his arm, calling his name even as she shook him.

Somehow, he finally managed to open his eyes.

And then he saw her bending over him, her blond hair falling into her face, her hand on his arm. Holding him and keeping him from falling.

Startled, he bolted upright.

The ravine, the churning waters, they were gone. He was back in his office again. The same office where he'd lain down a few minutes ago to catch a short nap before driving himself home.

No, wait, it wasn't a few minutes ago. It was last night.

Except that, unlike last night, he wasn't alone. Ramona Tate was looking down at him, concern evident in her sky-blue eyes.

"Are you all right?" she asked, and he realized that this wasn't the first time he'd heard the question. She'd voiced it before, only then it had been part of his dream—or maybe he should start calling it his nightmare. *Nightmare* seemed like a far more fitting label for it.

Sitting up, he swung his legs off the sofa, trying to gather his dignity to him.

"What are you doing here?" he asked gruffly, dragging his hand through his hair.

"It's eight o'clock," she told him politely. When he continued staring at her, she added, "You told me to come in early for a tour. Introduce me to some of the other people, things like that. I knocked on your door first," she added. "You didn't answer, but I heard you moaning."

Scrubbing his hand over his face, Paul tried to focus. "I was having a nightmare."

Ramona nodded. "That's what it sounded like," she agreed. Her eyes washed over him, taking in every last detail, or so it felt to him. What was she thinking? he couldn't help wondering. "You never went home last night, did you?"

"One of my patients called in, or rather, her husband did. She was spotting and really afraid. I met them at the hospital. I seem to have a calming effect on her and her husband," he added with a shrug. A pain zigzagged up and down his spine. He'd forgotten how uncomfortable his sofa really was.

"And?" Ramona prodded.

The woman actually looked interested, Paul mused. "She delivered just before midnight."

Her eyes held his. "Everything went all right?" she wanted to know.

He laughed shortly. "Other than the fact that the babies arrived six weeks prematurely and that Marc McGee fainted at the first sign of blood, everything went just fine."

"Babies?" she echoed. One of the allegations making the rounds against the Armstrong Fertility Institute was that there were entirely too many embryos being implanted at one time, resulting in multiple births. "How many babies?"

Was that interest, or suspicion, he heard in her voice? He wasn't sure. "She had twins. Two boys. I think she was hoping for one of each, but the last few hours, she was just hoping they'd be alive and well— and out of her."

Her mouth curved warmly. "So you delivered them and then came in here to catnap?"

Paul shrugged dismissively. "Something like that."

He still looked tired, Ramona thought. She wasn't going to ingratiate herself to him if he felt that he had to drag her around when he was half-asleep.

"Look, if you'd like to postpone my orientation and go home to catch up on your sleep, I understand completely. We can do this tomorrow," she told him cheerfully.

Paul rotated his shoulders, trying to get the kink out. The sofa had definitely *not* been constructed with napping in mind. Still, though she'd given him an out, he didn't want to postpone the tour. He'd already postponed it once when he shifted it from yesterday to today.

"Tomorrow," he told her, "has a habit of never coming."

Tongue in cheek, she pretended to take this as a revelation. "You know something that the newscasters don't?"

He wasn't sure if she was kidding or not. "I just meant that life has a habit of interfering with things. If we postpone this now, who knows what might come up tomorrow? For all I know, there might be a bigger fire to deal with." He stretched, feeling several muscles line up in protest as he did so. "Just give me a couple of minutes to pull myself together."

She was more than willing to be cooperative. "No problem. I can wait in my office if you like. And, better still," she volunteered, "I can get you a cup of coffee."

The offer out of left field surprised him. "I thought that women didn't do that anymore, get coffee for their boss."

Were her eyes smiling or laughing when she looked at him? He couldn't tell. "Women don't like being *told* to get coffee. Volunteering to do it is a whole different story." She leaned in closer to him for a moment. Close enough for him to get a heady whiff of her perfume.

Something remote stirred for a second, then faded. "And in case you didn't notice, I was volunteering. You take it black, don't you?"

"Is that a guess," he wanted to know, "or are you clairvoyant, too?"

"Just a guess," she assured him cheerfully. "The percentages were in my favor," she confided. "You don't strike me as the latte type, or even the cream-and-sugar type."

"I strike you as the black-coffee type," he said and she couldn't tell if she'd affronted him, or if he was just trying to figure out what that actually meant. He seemed to be the kind of person who needed to have everything in black and white. He was, she silently promised him, in for a surprise. But for the time being, she'd play things his way.

Ramona nodded. "Basic. Good, rich, no frills."

He realized that for a second, his breath had backed up into his lungs. That did it, no more sleeping on the office sofa.

"Are you describing the coffee or me?" He didn't realize until he heard the words that he had said them out loud.

She smiled in response and for a second, he didn't think she was going to answer. But then she grinned impishly and said, "Both," just before she left the office.

Paul sat there for a long moment, staring at the closed door. He needed to get his day going, he reminded himself, not try to figure out the puzzles that hid behind Ramona's sparkling eyes and long, shapely legs.

Crossing to the door, he locked it and then went to change into the spare suit he kept on hand.

A shower would have been nice, as well, but that was a luxury he couldn't afford right now. He had a full schedule today, which was why he'd suggested doing the orientation so early. These days, he thought as he swiftly changed clothes, he always felt as if he was half a league behind in his life.

Someday, he promised himself, he was going to catch up.

Ramona was just looking at her watch for a second time, wondering if Paul Armstrong had decided to postpone her orientation tour after all when she heard the light rap on her door.

Rather than bidding him to come in, she opened the door, thinking that was the friendlier path to take. She was trying everything in her power to build a bond between them. If she was going to get anywhere, she knew she needed to erase that suspicious glint that came into his eyes whenever he looked at her.

Her immediate goal was to put him at ease and get him to trust her. If she could accomplish that, everything else would fall into place, both her primary reason for being here and the one she'd given her editor, Walter Jessup, so that she'd have his blessing and backing to be here.

"Hi," she greeted Armstrong brightly as she opened the door. "I thought maybe you'd changed your mind or forgotten about me."

"Not much chance of that," he said, commenting on the last phrase.

Paul sincerely doubted that *anyone* could forget about Ramona Tate once they met her. She wasn't the kind of woman who, left unseen, would just fade into some nether field. She had the kind of face that lingered on a man's mind long after she'd walked away. *Long* after.

Closing the door again, Ramona produced a tall container of coffee, strong and hot, and held it out to him.

"Coffee, as promised," she said.

It smelled rich and delicious. He was willing to bet any amount of money that this coffee had definitely not emerged out of any of the vending machines located on the first floor. Or *any* of the other institute floors for that matter.

Tempted, he took a sip and savored the outstanding brew for a moment. "Where did you get this?"

Ramona gestured toward the machine. "I brought my own coffeemaker to work." The machine, which first ground whole beans and then brewed the results, was sitting on a file cabinet that, when the last occupant worked out of this office, had housed countless piles of books and papers. "This way, I don't have to drop everything to go find Starbucks."

That sounded incredibly dedicated.

"I'm sure that when he hired you, my brother didn't intend for you to be chained to your desk for hours at a time."

Ramona didn't respond to his statement. Instead, she seemed to be watching him intently as he paused to take another sip.

"So," she asked, her voice a tad lower and more melodic, "is it the way you like it?"

Jarred, Paul blinked and stared at her. He must have heard wrong. "Excuse me?"

"The coffee." She nodded at the container he held in his hand. "Is it the way you like it?"

"Oh." For a minute, he thought she was asking him if he—

Unconsciously shaking his head, Paul banished the thought that had popped unwittingly into his head.

"You didn't like it?" Ramona asked, trying to make sense out of the way he was reacting.

She looked disappointed. Was she that sensitive? Or was this all an act for some reason he couldn't quite fathom yet?

"No. I mean yes, I did. And no, that wasn't why I was shaking my head." It felt as if his thoughts were all scrambled and it was only partially due to his waking up so abruptly. "I'm just trying to get the last of the cobwebs out of my brain."

She smiled and indicated the container with her eyes. "If you finish the coffee, I think the cobwebs will self-destruct on their own. Oh." She said the words as if she suddenly remembered something. Before he could ask if she had, she answered his question. "I brought pastries." She flashed a grin and a little ray of sunshine entered the room. It was becoming a given. "In case you wanted something sweet to go along with your coffee."

The sweet thing that he found himself wanting to go along with his coffee hadn't come from any oven, but because he was hungry, he forced his thoughts to zero in on the practical.

Ramona was taking the box she'd brought out of the double drawer where she'd put it. Placing it on her desk, she took off the lid and pushed the box closer toward Paul. He took one small muffin and sat down in the chair facing her desk.

She took a seat, as well. "I'm guessing this sort of thing happens to you on a regular basis. Spending the night here," she added when Armstrong looked at her quizzically.

She was right, but he had no idea where she'd gotten her conclusion from. He doubted that very many people here took note of the fact that sometimes his hours threaded themselves well into the night if the situation called for it.

"What makes you say that?" he wanted to know.

"Your clothes. You changed," she pointed out when he looked down at what he was wearing. "You keep a change of clothing in your office or locker or whatever. That means you've slept in your office."

He saw no harm in admitting to her that she'd deduced correctly. "It's happened a few times," he acknowledged.

Armstrong seemed almost modest. She prided herself on being able to spot a phony. Could he actually be the genuine article?

"You must be very dedicated," she observed with what she felt was just the right touch of awe.

He didn't know if he'd call it dedicated. He did feel a sense of responsibility toward the people who came to his father's institute.

"The people who come here looking for help are desperate," he told her without any fanfare. "We're their last hope. You tend to feel responsible for them as well as to them. If I'm only available to them on a strict schedule or when it's convenient for me, then I have no business working in medicine. Punching a time clock is for people who work on an assembly line. I'm in a different line of work," he concluded quietly.

She studied him for a moment. "You do extraordinary things here, Paul. You help people conceive babies. Some would say that's God's line of work." She smiled warmly, keeping her tone nonjudgmental. "I guess what I'm wondering is if you sometimes feel, well, godlike." Her eyes raised to his and pressed innocently. "Well, do you?"

The whole idea was completely absurd.

"Never once," he informed her firmly. Finishing the pastry, he wiped his fingers on the napkin she'd supplied and finished the last of his coffee, dusted off a crumb from his jacket and then looked at her. "Are you ready to take that tour of the institute now?"

She was on her feet immediately, closing the lid on the pastry box and abandoning her own coffee. She raised her face to his and told him, "I was born ready."

Paul had no idea why he felt she wasn't really referring to the tour, but was, instead, putting him on some kind of notice.

But he did.

A warmth, joining forces with anticipation, washed over him. He banked it down, but his pulse continued marking time at a heightened beat that only seemed to increase the closer he walked beside Ramona.

Chapter Seven

The tour through the institute lasted close to an hour. Because he was pressed for time, Paul moved quickly throughout the modern three-story building. Ramona kept pace with him and peppered him with questions every step of the way. Endless, probing questions.

If he didn't know any better, Paul would have said that it felt as if he was under interrogation. He'd never encountered anyone who was so incredibly and relentlessly curious about the place in which she found herself employed.

He took her to see the various meeting rooms and then on to the boardroom. When they arrived, Ramona walked in before he could move on.

"My God, this is huge," she breathed, looking around in awe. It felt as if her voice was echoing in the cavernous room.

It made him think of Alice when she first took stock of Wonderland. Ramona even had the long blond hair.

Where had that thought even come from? He shouldn't be evaluating her looks—just her skills.

Ramona took it all in, moving around slowly. The room was wood paneled and had floor-to-ceiling windows. It was a sunny day and there were prisms of light bouncing off the walls and the very large, elegant oak conference table.

Paul watched, mesmerized despite himself, as Ramona spun around full circle beside the windows before turning to look at him.

"I think my apartment is smaller than this. Why do you need such a large conference room?" Before he could answer her, she made her own guess. "Is it to dwarf the egos that might be here?"

Being caught off guard by this woman was beginning to be an unfortunate habit. "What?"

"A room this large makes a person feel small," she explained. "That might be handy in getting people to do what you want them to."

"I have nothing to do with the size of this room," he told her. "That was my father's design."

His father had been the one to choose this location to begin with and he'd been involved in every phase of its construction. Despite the fact that he had not been part of it for a while now, the institute bore Gerald's indelible stamp and would always be his building, even long after the man was gone.

"I see," Ramona said thoughtfully as they both exited the room.

He didn't like the way she said that. "What is it that you see?"

Keep it low-key, Ramona. You don't want to push the man away or put him on his guard. "Just that your father must be a very forceful man."

"At the moment, he's a retired man." Paul thought about his father, about how withdrawn and, on occasion, bitter the man had become. The senior Armstrong hardly ever left the house now.

She knew that Gerald Armstrong was retired, but she was curious if he still kept a finger on the pulse of "his" clinic. For some men, *retirement* was just a meaningless word. "Does he ever come in and see how things are going?"

Initially, his mother had tried to get his father involved in the institute again. It seemed rather an ironic turn, seeing as how Gerald's obsession with the institute had taken such a heavy toll on their marriage in the beginning.

Paul thought Ramona would abort her line of questioning when he told her, "My father's in a wheelchair." He realized that he should have known better. The woman just kept going and going.

"That doesn't stop some people," Ramona said tactfully.

"It does others," he countered. They were making their way back to the elevators. He couldn't keep his curiosity in check any longer. "Why are you asking so many questions?"

She looked at him with an innocent expression that seemed to say that the answer was self-evident. "How else am I going to find things out? By the way," she continued, stepping into the elevator car, "where are the archives housed?"

He stared at her for a moment, then pressed for the next floor down. "In the basement. Why?"

The answer was tendered in utter innocence. The doors closed. "I thought I'd take a look at them when I got the chance."

In less than a minute, the elevator doors were opening again on the floor below. "Again, why?"

"To get a sense of the institute's history," she told him as they got off.

He had no desire to have her rummaging through the files that were stored down there. For the most part, they were charts and records that belonged to some of the institute's first patients. "If you have any questions, you can come to me."

He was walking faster, she noted, and lengthened her own stride. Was he just trying to get this over with, or was he subconsciously running from something?

"You just wanted to know why I'm asking so many

questions," she reminded him. "I don't want to bother you any more than I have to."

It might have seemed like a good idea to Derek at the time, but he was back to being sorry that his brother had talked him into letting Ramona stay. That was going to have to change and soon. He didn't particularly want Ramona Tate digging around, disrupting the rhythm of things.

"As far as I'm concerned," he told her as they went down the corridor, "this position is a one-shot deal. And you've fired the shot, or you will sometime today I imagine."

It was her turn to be confused, Ramona thought. "Come again?"

"The press release about Bonner and Demetrios joining our staff," he reminded her. "You wrote it. You'll deliver it if you haven't already. That's why my brother initially hired you."

"Initially." She picked up on the word he used and emphasized it. "But that was just the beginning, Dr. Armstrong."

Paul stopped walking and looked down at her, a man whose overnight guest had just announced she was settling in for the next six months. "Oh?"

Ramona continued walking as if she was oblivious to the fact that he had stopped. "The way I see it, the institute is in a precarious state, like a forest in the middle of a really hot summer. There are bound to be fires. It's my job to put those fires out."

He resumed walking. "And what if there are no fires?" he challenged.

"Then I'll have a very stress-free job." She slanted a look at him, more than a hint of a smile on her lips. "But do you really think that will be the case?"

He didn't want to dwell on "fires" or public relations or baseless rumors that were running amok. He just wanted to do his job. "All I want to do is help couples have the families they've always wanted."

She wanted to believe him, to believe that even in this modern, fast-paced world there were still people who wanted to do decent things out of the goodness of their heart. But until she disproved those rumors that she'd come to investigate, she couldn't allow herself to be taken in by the innocent look in his eyes.

"I understand, Dr. Armstrong, but things are never as simple as we'd like them to be. It's my job to make sure that you can do yours without being hampered by innuendo or, more important, lawsuits," she told him, deliberately presenting him with a cheerful demeanor. "Public opinion can either be a wonderful tool, or a weapon."

He stopped right in front of the lab. "How old are you?"

"Old enough to be good at what I do." It sounded like an evasive answer, but she didn't want to give him a direct answer. She knew that Armstrong was thirty-six and to him, she undoubtedly looked as if she was just out of elementary school.

"I was only thinking that you seemed awfully young to sound so cynical."

She didn't think of herself as cynical, but she let it go. Instead, she said, "These days, cynicism is built into the DNA."

With a sigh, Paul shook his head and then pushed open the door to their state-of-the-art lab. He was proud of the equipment, proud of all the advances they'd made in the field because they were able to afford the kind of cutting-edge research to be done here.

Holding the door, he allowed her to walk in ahead of him.

Like the conference room, the lab was one large room. Unlike the conference room, it had two tables instead of one. The tables were waist high, equipped with sinks and a number of microscopes that were hooked up to projection screens and computers. There were several people in the lab at the moment, all dressed in white coats.

She'd heard as well as read a great deal about the newly transplanted research team of Bonner and Demetrios before she ever came to the institute. Consequently, she knew them on sight.

Only Ted Bonner was present at the moment. Chance Demetrios had an office in the building. Her guess was that he was probably there now.

Bonner did strictly research. He had the luxury of divorcing himself from the people who ultimately made use of the end product of his research via one of the doctors on the staff. This allowed him to throw himself wholeheartedly into his work. His failures had no faces on them, but then, neither did his successes.

She heard Paul take in a breath, as if he was bracing himself for some kind of ordeal. The next moment, she realized that *she* was the ordeal.

"Dr. Bonner," he addressed the exceedingly tall, exceedingly good-looking dark-haired man who was about to bend over to look into one of the microscopes, "I would like to introduce you to Ramona Tate. She's our new public-relations manager."

Shaking her hand, Ted quipped, "I didn't know you had an old public-relations manager."

"We didn't," Paul answered before he realized that Ted was joking. "This is my brother's idea. He thinks we need protecting." He flashed a semiapologetic smile toward Ramona.

Thinking to spare him, she made no comment. She was getting a great many mixed signals from this man and decided it was better to pretend to be oblivious to all of them.

She turned her attention to the man who was still holding her hand enveloped in his. "Nice to meet you, Dr. Bonner. Would you mind if I got back to you later sometime? I'd like to ask you a few questions if I may."

"I'll be looking forward to it," Ted assured her. "Anything I can answer now?"

She slanted a glance toward Paul. "No," she assured Ted. "Not now."

"Then I'll get back to work," he said, releasing her hand.

"What do you want to talk to him about?" Paul asked her the moment they walked out of the lab. He didn't bother to try to hide the suspicious look on his face. What was she up to? he wondered. Were all these questions normal? Was he so out of touch with the way things worked outside his small sphere?

She was ready for him. "Well, for one thing, I want to know what enticed Dr. Bonner and his partner to come here to do their research."

They walked down the corridor, each with a different destination in mind. He to his other office and she back to hers. But for now, they walked together.

"The lab they came from wasn't exactly third rate or shabby by any means," Ramona continued. "And there's a certain amount of inherent prestige being associated with a teaching hospital–slash–college the caliber of the one they came from." She stopped walking. He stopped a second after that and looked at her, waiting. "Did you offer them more money?"

He made no answer, trying to gauge what, if anything, he should say. Maybe, if he just waited long enough, she'd go away. Silence ricocheted between them.

Ramona pressed her lips together. "Dr. Armstrong, you need to talk to me if I'm to do my job and do you any good."

"It was a little more money," Paul finally admitted to her.

The inflection in his voice told her there was more. "And?"

Paul drew himself up. It was a purely defensive move. Knights running to man the castle parapets. "And I gave them carte blanche." He shrugged carelessly. "I thought that having them here would negate any bad publicity that might have cropped up."

"Aggressively heading that publicity off at the pass accomplishes that," Ramona pointed out. "For starters, I need to get that press release—released," she concluded, humor curving her generous mouth.

He glanced at his watch, blinking once to focus in on it better. "I have a procedure to get to," he reminded her—and himself.

"Then I should get out of your way," Ramona responded amiably. "Thanks for the tour," she added.

As far as it went, Ramona added silently. She noticed that the good doctor had conspicuously left out the basement with its archives. But she wasn't put off. She was confident that she'd find a way to get into that one way or another. Ramona had a very strong feeling that was where she'd find what she was really looking for.

At least, she sincerely hoped so.

Nodding at Armstrong, she turned on her heel and quickly headed back to her office. She had work to do: theirs, her editor's and, the first moment she could find an island of time when no one was around to catch her, her own.

Paul stood like a pillar, watching her leave. With

effort, he roused himself. He had no time to stand here like some pubescent adolescent, watching her hurry away, he silently chastised. He had a reputation to uphold. That reputation included never being late, especially not for a procedure.

How the hell had things gotten so damn out of control?

The question echoed over and over again in Derek's brain, haunting him.

Taunting him.

It had all started out so innocently. So harmlessly. A simple weekend trip to Atlantic City. He was going to be staying at one of the more luxurious casinos and, if time permitted, he figured that he'd indulge in a little gambling.

How was he to know that things would mushroom into *this*—an obsession that would threaten to completely ruin his life?

He'd never seen it coming.

In his defense, he'd never even *felt* the inclination to gamble before. But that had been *before* the first incredible rush had found him.

There was no other way to describe the feeling that exploded in his veins when turn after turn of the card rendered him the big winner at the table. It was an exhilarating, overwhelming rush. The closest he had ever come to a religious experience.

By the end of that first evening, he was staring at more money than he ever had before. And it was *his* money. Not his father's, not his family's or the institute's, but *his*. Exclusively.

He wasn't just one of Gerald Armstrong's sons, or the CFO of the Armstrong Fertility Institute, an empty title awarded him because of who his father was. At that specific moment in time, he was Derek Armstrong. *Winner*.

And then, when he returned to the table the next night, as mysteriously as it had found him, his winning streak abandoned him. Hand after hand, he lost. Desperate to recapture that magical feeling, to see that life-affirming envy in the other players' eyes, he kept betting.

And he kept losing.

At the end of the weekend, he'd not only lost all the money he'd won, but he lost twice as much as he'd brought to Atlantic City.

He began signing notes, barking that he was good for it. His luck remained bad. He only won enough to remind him that it was possible. Just not probable.

Eventually, the house stopped accepting his markers. That was when someone else did. And his life took a turn for the worse.

Addled by his desire to recoup his losses and to prove that his groundless certainty that he could win it all back if he just kept at it long enough was right, he went on to accept the loan for a large sum of money. The loan had come from a well-dressed, older man with the flattest eyes he'd ever seen.

And now, now he was in so far over his head that

he despaired he would ever break through the surface again. Lying on top of the rumpled bed in the shabby Atlantic City hotel room, he dragged both hands over his face in abject despair.

What was he going to do?

The demands for payments were relentless. And the threats, the threats frightened him most of all. Not just against his life, but against his parents and the institute, as well.

The threats hadn't been in so many words, but when he was late with his third payment, a payment that had become swollen out of proportion because the interest that had been slapped on it grew at a prodigious rate, his "benefactor"—as the man had referred to himself at first—quietly slipped him a news clipping. The clipping was from a West Coast newspaper from approximately six months ago. The photograph that was at the top of the article showed a once-famous hotel going up in flames.

"The owner of that piece of property didn't think he had to pay on time, either," was all the man said to him in that raspy voice that came across like a poor imitation of Marlon Brando in *The Godfather*.

Derek never asked who the benefactor was referring to. He didn't want to know. The lesson was crystal clear. If he didn't continue to pay off his loan on time, the institute would be burned to the ground.

He sold everything he owned and still, it wasn't enough. Having nothing left, immersed in maintaining a facade, Derek was left with only one source of money to tap. He handled the institute's finances. So he set aside his conscience and did what he had to do.

It was either that or watch the institute burn.

He refused to think of the consequences of his actions, but he knew they were coming.

And soon.

In the meantime, he would continue to burn the candle at both ends, trying to stay alive one more day. Hoping that, at the end of the day, there would be some kind of miracle that could save him. It was the only way he could go on. Searching for a miracle. And praying that his luck had changed.

Chapter Eight

Paul had to admit that the press release looked even better in newsprint than it had on the antiseptic white pages that Ramona had handed him to read several days ago.

He put down the first section of the *Cambridge Chronicle*. The periodical had been sitting on his desk when he'd walked in this morning, opened to the page with the pertinent article on it.

Aside from the Donner-Demetrios announcement, there was mention of the clinic's high success ratio, and the article brought attention to the fact that, not all that long ago, the institute was first of its kind to offer hope to childless, infertile couples longing for a baby of their own.

The article ended by emphasizing that the institute was still on the cutting edge of the field, still leading the way. Hiring Bonner and Demetrios to conduct their research at the institute just ensured that they would continue on that path.

"So, has she earned her keep?"

Derek walked into his office grinning and looking extremely satisfied with himself. Paul wasn't aware that his brother had even bothered to knock.

"Did you leave this on my desk?" he wanted to know, indicating the newspaper.

That possibility hadn't occurred to him until Derek had asked the question. He'd just assumed that Ramona had left the paper to prove to him that she was doing her job.

"Had to," Derek responded. Rather than take a seat, he perched on the corner of the cluttered desk. It created the aura of looking down on his brother. Paul had a feeling Derek did it on purpose. "You walk around here the way you do through life, with blinders on. Not seeing anything until it's pointed out to you." Derek's grin grew wider. "I bet you didn't even notice that our new PR manager is one hell of a babe, did you?"

That's where you're wrong, Derek.

Whether or not his brother meant his question in a belittling way, he couldn't help resenting the way Derek said it.

"I noticed that she was a very attractive woman," Paul answered, "but I wouldn't have insulted her by describing her in those terms."

Derek shook his head. "Don't know how we can possibly share the same DNA and be so damn different."

"One of the mysteries of science, I guess," Paul replied coolly. Derek continued smirking at him. "And if you're here to gloat—"

"I am," Derek confirmed breezily.

Paul refused to rise to the bait. "One success doesn't make your case for you."

Derek stared at him, clearly surprised by this opposition. "Don't tell me you still want to get rid of her."

"What I'm telling you is that I'm still reserving judgment." Other places had a three-month period during which a newly hired employee could be let go if he or she didn't live up to expectations or performed poorly. Why not here at the institute, as well? "I see this place as being a tightly knit family. I'm not convinced that she belongs yet."

Derek laughed shortly, clearly not in agreement with his twin. "That's exactly your problem, Paul. The institute isn't a family, it's a business and as such, it needs to have people savvy about their particular sphere of business running it." Rising, he patted Paul on the shoulder. Paul pulled back from his brother's patronizing gesture. "But that's not your concern. You just go on doing you job and I'll make sure that you can *keep* on doing it."

Paul wasn't as dense as he assumed his brother thought him to be. He saw through the rhetoric. "I'm not handing over my right to challenge your decisions, if that's what you're after."

Derek pretended to snap his fingers like an old-fashioned villain and declared in a pseudoexasperated voice, "Curses, foiled again."

Paul relaxed just a little. "You're in a particularly chipper mood today."

Derek's grin broadened even more. "Why shouldn't I be? The sun is smiling down on our institute and all is right with the world." And then he added the crowning piece. "And I feel lucky."

Paul didn't understand what his brother might be referring to. "Lucky?"

"Lucky to be part of all this," Derek said, neatly smoothing out the unfortunate slip he'd just accidentally made.

Last night he'd left the table slightly better off than when he'd first walked into the casino. It was the beginning of a streak, he could feel it. He'd flown back to Cambridge early this morning, but he intended on going back again as soon as he was able to delegate his responsibilities for the upcoming weekend. He didn't want his streak to get cold.

"By the way," Derek interjected, stopping at the door just before leaving the office, "have you told her you liked the article?"

"I gave it my approval initially," he said evasively.

Derek continued staring at him. "I haven't had time to talk to anyone but you," Paul protested. "I haven't even left my office yet."

"Then leave it and go tell her," Derek prompted. "Everyone needs a little positive reinforcement once in a while. I'm guessing that you haven't given her any substantial feedback. I don't want to risk losing the woman to someone else—even if you do."

He hated it when Derek insisted on putting words into his mouth or second-guessing his thoughts. "That's not necessarily true," Paul contradicted.

"Such passion," Derek quipped, placing his hand over his heart. "Well, you've convinced me."

Paul held his tongue. Sarcasm wasn't something he indulged in with any sort of regularity, but his brother seemed to have cornered the market for both of them.

"I'll see you later," he told Derek, hoping that would help usher his brother out the door.

Derek paused again, his hand on the doorknob. "As a matter of fact, you won't. I have some unfinished business to tend to," he said evasively.

According to Derek, he had just been in New York. Unfinished business would indicate that he was returning there. "You're flying back to New York?"

"Yes."

His brother seemed antsy to leave now, but Paul still wanted to find out what was prompting all these trips. Was Derek involved with someone in the city? Or was there something else going on? "Mind if I ask why? You were just there."

Derek had his explanation ready. "I'm trying to hit up some corporate types for donations to the institute. That requires wining and dining and a lot of kid-glove attention, something you wouldn't know anything about," he pointed out, "because I take that burden off your shoulders."

That still didn't make any sense to Paul. "I thought that was why the institute holds several different annual fundraisers each year."

Derek sighed wearily. He'd never liked having to explain himself, especially when things were not quite what they seemed. "In case you haven't noticed, the price of everything is going up. If the institute was a play, I'd say we needed angels backing it," he explained, thinking that the metaphor was lost on his brother.

Paul let the hint of sarcasm pass. There was no point in taking offense. It wouldn't resolve anything. Another sigh, this time one that had nothing to do with impatience, escaped.

"Yes, we need angels," Paul murmured, more to himself than to Derek. Dealing in the creation of tiny beings was more in the domain of angels than anything else, he thought.

Derek had taken the opportunity to make good his exit.

Paul half rose in his seat. "Let me know how it goes," he called after his brother. Derek merely waved an acknowledgment without looking back.

* * *

"Good piece."

At the sound of Paul's voice, Ramona's heart jumped into her throat. She hadn't expected anyone to walk in and she was busy doing research on the institute and its founder, Gerald Armstrong. Caught off guard, doing her best to look surprised rather than guilty, it took her a second to compose herself.

"Excuse me, Doctor?"

"I saw the press-release article you wrote about Bonner and Demetrios in the *Chronicle*," he explained as he came in. "Nice to see something in the newspaper about the institute without veiled accusations running through it."

Ramona's response was a knowing smile. Barely moving her hand so that she wouldn't call any attention to it or the monitor facing her, she deftly pressed down on a combination of keys that brought up a neutral screen. She had a feeling that the doctor wouldn't exactly be thrilled if he knew she'd been researching those very articles.

It looked as if she and Armstrong were finally getting on better footing. She needed to feed that. "By the time I get finished working on the institute's image, people are going to think of it as being on the same plane as the Grotto of Lourdes."

"Setting your sights a little high, aren't you?" he asked, amused.

She had never approached life any other way. "If

you set your sights too low, you never get to accomplish anything noteworthy. Life is a series of challenges. You're not going to meet them if you're sitting on the sidelines," she told him.

He turned her words over in his head and then laughed.

Was he laughing at her? She'd thought he was too polite and well mannered for that. "What's so funny, Doctor?"

"I just can't picture you on the sidelines of *anything*," he told her honestly.

For a second, she was silent. And then she said, "Thank you," very quietly. "Do you realize that's the first time you've given me a compliment?"

He didn't want her to get carried away. "It's not meant as a compliment," he felt bound to tell her. "It's just an observation."

Another man would have taken advantage of that, she thought. Apparently *honorable* wasn't just a word in the dictionary to Dr. Armstrong. That definitely made him different from his father. So far, she'd compiled a rather formidable pile of dirt on the senior Armstrong, who'd been a womanizer—and there was enough to go around as far as Derek Armstrong was concerned. But she was after more than that. She wanted to find something that would substantiate the notion that Gerald had played fast and loose with patients' eggs and sperm, at times possibly even substituting an egg or sperm from donors rather than his patients. So far, she had nothing concrete.

And as for Paul, she hadn't uncovered *anything* on him yet. Not even a whisper of any sort of scandal much less wrongdoing. Either he was very, very good at hiding his tracks—or he was clean.

She was beginning to lean toward the latter.

"Well, I'm taking it as a compliment," she told him. An impulse hit her. Ramona glanced at her watch. It was only eleven. Early by most standards, but she'd been up since five. "You have any consultations or procedures set up?"

The question, coming out of the blue, caught him by surprise. "For when?"

"Now."

What was she driving at? he wondered. He'd come in early to catch up on some paperwork and to review several trials that had been conducted on a new kind of medication that just might be able to help with fertility. There were no appointments on his calendar today.

"No. Not until later."

"Good, then." Ramona rose to her feet. Ingrained manners had him rising, as well. "I'm taking you to lunch." She saw him look at his own watch. "An early lunch," she amended before he could protest that it wasn't officially lunchtime. "My treat." She took her purse out of the drawer where she kept it. "You can't turn me down. I'm celebrating."

Had he missed something? Or was the woman talking about the article making it into print? "Celebrating what?"

Her eyes crinkled when she smiled, he noticed. And she was smiling enough to light up two rooms. "My boss just gave me my first compliment," she told him cheerfully.

The woman was making entirely too big a deal out of this. "Ms. Tate—"

"Oh now, don't go spoiling it by going all formal on me," she chided him. "I've been here more than a week. Certainly that's long enough for you to remember my first name."

"I remember your first name," Paul protested. "It's just that—"

She wouldn't allow him to finish. "Good, then you can use it."

He found himself laughing and shaking his head. "Are you always this pushy?"

There wasn't even a moment's hesitation on her part. "Always," she confirmed. "I find I get more things done that way."

And with that, she led the way out of the office.

"So, how do you like working at the institute?" Ramona asked once they were seated at a table in Stella's, the quaint Italian restaurant a block or two from the clinic. The food was as old-fashioned as the decor and just as tasty as the aroma drifting in from the kitchen promised it would be.

The server took their orders and retreated, leaving them with bread sticks that were out of this world.

"Shouldn't I be the one asking you that?" Paul wanted to know, looking at her. Her hair looked somewhat darker in the dim light. It was medium gold instead of bright blond, Paul caught himself thinking. Either way, it was incredibly attractive.

"I already know how I feel about working at the institute," she answered. "But you must have had a hard time, trying to walk in your father's shoes." Her eyes were on his, looking for a reaction as she said, "If I had to guess, I'd say that Gerald Armstrong was a hard act to follow."

He shrugged. "I just try to do justice to his vision."

Paul loved his father, she realized, and couldn't help wondering if that affection was returned, or if the senior Armstrong had been too wrapped up in his work and in the women who'd fawned on him over the years to even realize the precious thing he was ignoring.

She bit off a piece of bread stick, then asked as nonchalantly as she could, "And, in your opinion, have you succeeded?"

His eyes narrowed as he picked up a bread stick of his own. "I thought you were asking me out to lunch, not an interview."

She needed to dial it back a little, Ramona told herself. She had a tendency to come on strong. That would be a mistake here.

"This isn't an interview," she told him innocently. "I'm just trying to get a few things more clear so that I can tell your story better when I get around to writing it."

He straightened, abandoning the last of the bread stick. "Tell my story to whom?"

"To the general public," she answered. "I was thinking of putting together a piece on the institute. You know, on how it came about, the changes that were implemented when you and your brother and sister took over, things like that. I want to send it to one of the papers that has a Sunday magazine. Part of the reason you have to put up with rumors and detractors is that not enough people understand what it is you do. I think that too many of them regard you as being on the same level as Dr. Frankenstein—trying to create life out of thin air and coming up with Boris Karloff."

He couldn't say that he liked the idea of being dissected in public, or even held up to scrutiny. Not because he had anything to hide, but because he was and always had been a private person. The spotlight was for people like his father and Derek. They enjoyed it. He just wanted to be left alone to do his work.

But for now, he made no protest. He could always do that later. "Who else have you interviewed?"

"No one." Which was true. She was relying on sources for that. "I thought I'd start at the top and work my way down."

Their food arrived, the aromas enticing them to start eating.

"If that's the case," Paul said, continuing where they had left off, "you probably should have started with Derek."

She waited until she'd taken a bite before contradicting him. "Derek's not at the top, you are." Then, in case he didn't understand her criteria, she told him, "Derek might be the chief financial officer, but you're the heart of the institute, Dr. Armstrong."

This was the first time anyone had ever accused him of having a heart, much less infusing its blood into the lifeline of the family business. It both pleased and embarrassed him.

"I'm hardly that," Paul told her, punctuating his words with a careless shrug.

"Oh, but you are," Ramona insisted. She smiled as she watched him shift in his seat. She was a student of body language. "I'm sorry, I didn't mean to embarrass you."

He wasn't about to confirm or deny that she had. "I'm just not accustomed to talking about myself."

"You weren't," she pointed out. "I was. So how *did* it feel, stepping into your father's shoes?" she pressed.

He thought of that first time, when he realized that he was flying solo. That his father was no longer there, making every decision, large or small, without consulting any of them. His father, in his eyes, had been a brilliant dictator.

"A little unnerving," Paul admitted quietly before he could think better of it and keep his own counsel.

Ramona nodded. "I would imagine. Did you ever want to override one of your father's accepted methods, but you hesitated because you felt he'd disapprove?"

Paul laughed quietly. He'd spent the entire first year constantly second-guessing himself. "Only every hour of every day."

"Well, the statistics I've seen so far seem to say that your success ratio is very, very high."

Ramona bit back the impulse to ask if that was due to implanting too many viable embryos. It was too soon to be that honest. She had to get him to trust her a bit more before she went after answers to questions like that.

But she couldn't help anticipating.

Chapter Nine

Looking back, in Paul's estimation lunch had gone by much too quickly.

Instead of being eager to make a hasty retreat, the way he'd anticipated when Ramona had first extended the invitation to him, he found himself wanting to linger even after the plates had been cleared away and the coffee was all but gone.

Which made no sense because he did have paperwork to catch up on. And besides, he'd never liked being subjected to questions, and lunch had been fairly littered with them, although she'd presented them amicably. Despite his natural tendency toward privacy and aversion to talking about himself, there was just something, some nebulous "thing" he couldn't put his finger on or explain, that had him enjoying this vibrant woman's company.

And wanting more.

"I guess we'd better go," she told him when the server finally cleared away their coffee cups. "You've probably got a full schedule this afternoon."

Ramona signaled for the check and when it arrived, he reached for it. She was faster and all but stole it right out from under his hand.

"I said it was my treat, remember?" Ramona reminded him.

His had always been a life of privilege. He wasn't accustomed to having someone else pay, especially not someone who was in his employ.

"Yes, but—"

Ramona guessed at what he was going to say. "You didn't think I meant it." She grinned as she continued, "Or is it that in the world you come from, men still pick up the tab no matter what?"

He didn't know if she was laughing at him, or just flashing another one of her incredibly sunny smiles. He would have liked to think it was the latter. "Perhaps a little of both," he allowed quietly.

"Well, I did mean it," she told him. "So you're going to have to adjust your thinking a little about the roles of men and women."

"You don't earn enough to toss money around like that," he pointed out.

That meant he'd reached for the check because he was being thoughtful. She wondered if Armstrong even realized that.

She offered a compromise. "Tell you what, I'll let you pay the next time."

Next time.

The words hung in the air like a red banner. As in going out to a restaurant again. Together. When had this been taken for granted? Paul felt as if he'd somehow grabbed hold of one of those horses on a merry-go-round and someone had upped the speed, making the carousel go faster and faster and preventing him from getting off.

Maybe he'd heard wrong.

"Next time?" he repeated.

"Next time," she affirmed. "As in some other time after this."

She'd unnerved him, Ramona realized. Paul Armstrong, in his own way, was rather sweet and sheltered, she decided. He was like a throwback to another century despite the fact that he was only eleven years older than she was.

The man was, she mused, utterly unlike his brother, and she was beginning to think that wasn't such a good thing—at least, not for her. Being in his company had a very strange way of blurring her parameters. She was going to have to watch that and keep sight of her priorities, Ramona silently chided as she surrendered her credit card to the waiter.

* * *

Going out to lunch with Ramona had thrown Paul off schedule, not to mention him, as well. Consequently, when he returned to the institute, he planned to stay and catch up on paperwork long after everyone else had left.

At least, that was his plan when he walked back into his office, but it slowly wound up changing over the course of the afternoon, as he caught himself thinking about his parents more than once. Especially his father.

That was Ramona's fault, he thought grudgingly. Her cheerful but endless questions had touched on his childhood and focused more than once on his father. That and the fond way she'd spoken of her own mother the rare time or two that the conversation had veered away from all things institute and shifted to her.

He caught himself envying her for the close relationship she shared with her mother. From what she'd told him, Ramona had grown up at a severe disadvantage, with a mother who frequently had to work two jobs in order to provide for things that he and his brother and sisters had taken for granted.

But no amount of privilege would outweigh the love Ramona had had while growing up, and from the sound of it, continued to have to this day. Paul and his siblings were closer to each other than to either parent. Their father seemed to always be away, busy at the institute or off to numerous conferences. Their mother never picked up the slack. Instead, she'd been distant, occupied with her society friends and obsessed with looking as if she had cornered the fountain of youth for her own private use.

If either parent took any notice of any of them, it was Gerald, who appeared to be marginally partial to Derek. Paul had a feeling that the founder of the fertility institute saw himself in Derek. Both were outgoing and outspoken—and very flirtatious, even silver-tongued. Paul knew he didn't possess any of these traits and that made him all but invisible to his father.

Listening to Ramona speak fondly of her mother, Paul found himself wishing that he had favorable memories of his parents to draw on in times of stress. Sure, he'd always loved them. But he had no illusions about the sentiment being returned. He knew that it was a one-way street.

He needed to do something to change that. Maybe he could begin with a little more close contact with both parents. It had been a while since he'd been back to the house where he and his siblings had grown up. It was more like a mausoleum than a home, but that didn't change the fact that he was long overdue for a visit.

The silent debate went back and forth for a while. Finally, just as the clock approached five, Paul powered down his computer and left.

Ramona, who was just getting off the elevator located on the far side of the corridor, saw him walk out the front entrance.

And made a mental note of it.

* * *

Maybe he should have called ahead, Paul thought as he approached the winding driveway. His parents might be entertaining and then he would be guilty of crashing their party.

But there were no valets racing back and forth, parking expensive automobiles. There wasn't even a single vehicle parked before the edifice that could only be described as a mansion. From the looks of it, his parents were alone.

That was in keeping with what was becoming, more and more, his father's reclusive nature.

For a moment, Paul thought of turning around and just going home.

But he was here now, he might as well stay, he told himself. Nothing was ever going to change if he didn't make an attempt to change it. Waiting for either of his parents to make the first move would only be an exercise in futility.

Leaving his vehicle parked in the driveway, he walked up to the three-story front doors and rang the bell. Several minutes later—long enough for him to think about leaving again—the door opened.

Anna, the Armstrongs' longtime housekeeper, looked surprised and then pleased to see him. "Well, hello," the older woman said warmly. Her eyes fairly sparkled as she smiled.

"I know," Paul responded as he walked in past her. "It's been a while."

"I was just thinking how nice it was to see you, Dr. Paul." The small, squat woman who had once been his nanny and had graduated to her present position when the old housekeeper retired, silently closed the door. "Your parents are in the front living room," she informed him. "Together for once," she added.

There was no judgment in her voice. It was just a simply stated fact. An unusual one since even when he was growing up, his parents were rarely in the same room at the same time, unless it was for a public function or there was a photographer involved.

"Thank you, Anna. You're looking well."

The woman smiled gratefully. "I'm looking older, but thank you for that. Will you be staying for dinner, Dr. Paul?"

He glanced toward the living room. The doors were opened, but at this distance, he couldn't see in. "Depends on how this plays out."

"I'll put up a plate," Anna told him confidently.

Lengthening his stride, Paul crossed to the living room. He stopped just short of the doorway, then quietly looked in.

Situated on opposite sides of the room, neither his mother nor his father seemed to notice him. Or each other, for that matter.

Theirs had been a marriage of inconvenient convenience. Gerald Armstrong had married Emily Stanton because he wanted a wife on his arm who had a pedigree and brought a considerable amount of money to the merger. Emily had married Gerald because even though the dynamic young doctor was socially beneath her, he was exciting and a future with him promised to be the same.

They'd both been disappointed in their expectations, but for the sake of appearances remained together. At least in theory.

As Paul stood there, silently studying these two people whose blood ran through his veins, his mother, beautifully groomed as always with every hair in place, was the first to notice him. If she was taken aback by his unannounced appearance, she covered it skillfully.

"Paul, what are you doing here?" Crossing to him, she brushed the air beside his cheek with a kiss. The same kiss she shared when greeting friends who weren't really friends. Stepping back, she appraised her son, searching for some kind of telltale sign of trouble. Artfully penciled eyebrows rose just the slightest fraction. "Is something wrong?"

He shook his head and forced a shadow of a smile to his lips. "Nothing's wrong, Mother. I just realized this afternoon that I hadn't been by for a while and thought I'd drop in on my way home."

His father, seated in the wheelchair he regarded as his prison, turned sharply away from the fireplace and looked at him.

"I'm not dead yet, if that's why you're here," Gerald snapped at his son.

"Didn't think you were, Dad," Paul said, keeping his voice mild as he came closer.

He went through a minor adjustment period every time he saw his father like this. Gerald Armstrong had been a giant of a man, both physically and in stature. But now, he seemed to have folded into himself, a whispered memory of the man he'd once been. All that was left was a booming voice that somehow seemed misplaced, as if it belonged to someone else and Gerald was just borrowing it for a little while.

Taking a breath, Paul tried to lighten the atmosphere a little. He smiled at his father and said, "Someone has a birthday coming up."

"Everyone has a birthday coming up," Gerald responded, scowling darkly. "Unless they have the good fortune to be dead."

Emily Armstrong waved away her husband's sour comment, then deliberately turned her back on Gerald and addressed her words to her son.

"Don't pay any attention to him. He's been in a mood all week. You have no idea what I've had to put up with." She sighed dramatically, her longing for the life she'd once led evident in every word she spoke. "I'm beginning to think I liked him better when he was busy with his work and his women."

Paul's eyes widened. He remembered the rumors, remembered, too, hearing Derek tell him that he'd made a play for their father's mistress after the senior

Armstrong had grown tired of her. Emily had been in the next room and Paul, horrified, had ordered Derek to shut up. He'd been foolish enough to think no one else knew about their father's wandering eyes and grasping hands, least of all their mother.

Even so, her comment caught him off guard. "Mother!"

To his surprise, his mother laughed. "You look stunned, Paul. What? You think I didn't know? That I believed all those stories of his about having to go off to conferences? *No one* goes to that many conferences," she jeered.

"You never said anything," Paul tried to explain.

Emily shrugged, turning her attention back to the liquor cabinet. Taking out a bottle of aged scotch, she poured the deep amber liquid into a glass. She took a long sip and savored the first taste for a moment before answering.

"I never said anything because there was no point in talking about it." And even if there was, she wouldn't have mentioned it to a child. Looking at her son's face, Emily anticipated what was going on in his orderly mind. He needed convincing. "There's a difference between not knowing and not caring." She slanted a glance at the man who was no longer handsome, no longer held any kind of attraction for her. "Sadly, I stopped caring a long time ago."

"What are you two whispering about over there?" Gerald demanded. Not waiting for an answer, he pressed one of the buttons on his right armrest. The automated chair instantly brought him right to them.

"Nothing that concerns you, Gerald," Emily answered evasively for the sake of peace. It was obvious she didn't want another scene.

"I don't believe you," Gerald snapped.

The evening degenerated from there.

Paul left right after dinner, feeling he'd done enough penance for one day. Possibly for a month.

It seemed to Paul that over the course of the next week and a half, Ramona Tate appeared to be everywhere. Their paths crossed at least half a dozen times a day. It got to a point that he was beginning to wonder if perhaps she had a global positioning satellite planted somewhere on his person that enabled her to find him wherever he went.

The thing of it was, he was beginning to look forward to seeing her.

Toward the end of the following week, Paul finally commented about it to Ramona. He tried not to make it seem as if he was calling her out on it, but he wanted an explanation. It almost seemed like too much of a coincidence.

When he walked into her as he was about to go into the lab and she was coming out, he said, "Our paths keep crossing."

The comment seemed to surprise her. "Now that you mention it, I noticed that, too."

"How do you explain it?" he asked, curious.

"Small building?" she offered with a beguiling smile. "There aren't that many places to go and since I can't really do my job sitting in my office for eight hours straight, per force I have to be mobile." Her mouth curved in that grin he had realized he looked forward to seeing far more than he should. "What's your excuse?" she wanted to know.

He stared at her, befuddled. Had she just turned the tables on him? "For what?"

"For turning up every place I am," she told him with a shrug.

The gesture was innocent and beguiling. The silky peasant blouse she wore slipped down her shoulder. She tugged it back in place under his watchful eye. He told himself he shouldn't be staring, but he couldn't look away.

"I don't know, you tell me." And then she pretended to hazard her own theory. "Maybe you decided you'd like to get to know me better and you don't know how to go about doing it."

He stared, stunned. "Ramona—Ms. Tate—" Words failed him.

She came to his rescue. "Relax, Dr. Armstrong. I'm only kidding," she teased. "I already told you, it's a small building. It's all coincidence. Now, if you'll excuse me, I have to take a trip up to the third floor." Stepping into the elevator he'd just vacated a few moments ago and that had been standing at the ready, she pressed the button for the third floor. "I have an appointment to talk to Dr. Bonner."

A score of red flags seemed to suddenly pop up in his head, as if warning him that something was off. Something was wrong.

"What are you planning on talking to him about?" he wanted to know.

"About his work, of course," she answered.

What kind of questions was she planning on asking the man? He thought that the threat of unrest was over. The article she'd written had appeared almost two weeks ago and since then, he'd heard no more rumors. Everything seemed to be fine.

So why was she talking to Bonner and who knew who else?

The last thing he saw before the silver doors closed was the expression on Ramona's face. She was smiling at him, but the look in her eyes was unfathomable. And that made him nervous.

Chapter Ten

It was hard to think of a mere thirty-eight-year-old as a science wunderkind, but that was exactly what the medical community had dubbed Ted Bonner. Even his detractors thought he was brilliant and his cheering section went on endlessly not just about his incredible mental acuity, but about his dark good looks, as well.

Ramona had always thought that intelligent, cerebral types came in dull shades of brown and gray. After being at the institute just a short while, she realized that she was definitely going to have to reassess the way she thought.

Though extremely busy, Bonner had agreed to pause for a few minutes and answer "just a few of your questions."

"A few is better than none," Ramona responded cheerfully. "Let's start with how the Armstrong Fertility Institute managed to entice you and Dr. Demetrios into leaving the university to join the staff here."

His mouth quirked in a smile. "Paul Armstrong said we could have carte blanche at the institute. That no one would interfere with our research and all he asked was to be given updates whenever we felt there was something noteworthy to share."

She noted that one of the lab technicians slowed her pace as she passed the good doctor. He was a heart stopper, all right, Ramona silently agreed.

"And how did this agreement with Mr. Armstrong differ from your previous employer?"

He laughed at the question. "The difference is like night and day. Previously, we were faced with a myriad of restrictions. It's a wonder we made any progress at all." Her puzzled look silently prompted him to elaborate. "Universities are *very* PC oriented. Or, more to the point, they're very fearful of being sued for one reason or another. They had all sorts of restrictions, rules and protocols for us to follow. And the massive amount of paperwork we had to do took away from actual lab time," he complained.

She watched his face for a telltale reaction as she stated her conclusion. "Then you and Dr. Demetrios must really be thrilled to be here."

He averted his eyes, glancing at something on the table before him when he answered, "Close to it."

Ramona read between the lines. "But?"

Again, he laughed. This time it was in self-deprecation. "Chance claims I wouldn't be satisfied in heaven," he said, referring to his research partner. "That I'd insist on rearranging the clouds if nothing else was off."

She could feel her pulse rate increasing. It took effort to keep the excitement out of her voice. "And what's off here?" she asked innocently.

He shifted his six-foot-four frame like a man who didn't want to be pinned down just yet. "I've got some reservations about the lab's protocols," he replied vaguely.

Again her eyes caught his. Was he guarding a secret, or was he just in the beginning stages of formulating his suspicions? And if so, what was he suspicious of? "For instance?"

Bonner let the bait pass him by. "I need to do a little more research into that before I feel comfortable enough to be more specific."

Damn it. So near and yet so far. She didn't want to give up, but she knew that she couldn't press too hard, either.

"It helps to talk things through," she encouraged. "You know, kind of like brainstorming. Maybe it's all just a misunderstanding...." Her voice trailed off as she mentally crossed her fingers.

But Bonner merely shrugged. "Maybe," he allowed. She could tell by his tone that he wasn't convinced—

but he wasn't about to say anything more, either. "But we each have our own way of doing things."

"No argument there." Although she'd dearly love to argue him out of this stance he'd taken. "Tell me, is it something that the institute has always done, or is it some new protocol?"

"Don't know the answer to that, either," Bonner admitted. "Most likely everything'll be cleared up once I go through the archives—if I ever get the chance to get down there." A timer went off, stealing his attention. Her time was up. "I've really got to get back to my work. If you'll excuse me?"

It wasn't a question, it was a statement, meant to politely usher her out.

Bonner obviously didn't want anyone looking over his shoulder as he worked, she thought. She could understand that.

"Of course." She closed the black leather-bound notebook she'd been taking notes in. "And thank you for your time."

But she was already talking to the back of his head as Bonner went to retrieve material from an incubator. Ramona quietly slipped out of the lab, passing several more techs scurrying about like mice.

The archives again, she thought as she got on the elevator. This just reinforced her desire to get into that basement room.

She was working on that, pressing for the first floor. She'd done her very best to be seen by as many people as she could so that everyone would come to regard her as a fixture here and wouldn't question her presence anywhere within the institute. Like the archives. It was time for her to find out just how she went about getting access to it.

Instead of going to her office when she got off on the first floor, Ramona took a detour and stopped by the medical clinic. Pushing open one of the glass doors, she walked into the waiting area. The large room was crowded to the limit with couples who were returning for procedures, there for counseling or coming in for the first time.

Looking at them, Ramona found that she couldn't tell one set from the other. Everyone had basically the same kind of expression, the kind of expression found on the faces of children on Christmas Eve, as they stared up at the skies and hoped that magic would briefly touch their lives and make their fondest wish come true.

"Lost?"

The softly voiced question came from behind her. She turned to see the clinic's receptionist sitting at her desk, watching her.

Wilma Goodheart had been at the institute practically from the very beginning and now, with the senior Dr. Armstrong gone, she regarded herself as its resident expert and historian. In her late fifties, she was the picture of the eternal, ever-efficient secretary.

"No, actually, I'm not," Ramona said, turning completely around to face her. "I came to ask you a question." Had Wilma not been loyal to a fault when it came to Gerald Armstrong and, by extension, his family, she would have actually had a ton of questions to ask the older woman. But since Wilma *was* loyal, she knew she would get nothing out of her that even hinted at the institute's secrets. "If I wanted to get some information from the archives, how would I go about it?" she asked, keeping her expression as innocent-looking as possible.

"You'd need a pass card to access the records room."

That sounded simple enough. But Ramona knew better than to be too confident. She took another tentative step across the semifrozen lake. At any moment, the older woman could grow suspicious and refuse to answer. "How do I get one of those?"

Wilma pursed her lips, something she always did when she was thinking. "What is it you want from there? Maybe I could—"

Ramona was quick to cut the woman off. "I don't want to impose on anyone. Besides, I'm not sure I know what I'm looking for yet."

Wilma scrutinized her, a hint of suspicion entering her brown eyes. "Then how will you know if you found it?"

"I'll know," Ramona told her with certainty. "It's just background information," she quickly added. "Maybe even the name of Dr. Gerald's first patient—"

"That's confidential," Wilma told her firmly. "I'm surprised that working in public relations, you don't know that."

"I'd use another name," she quickly assured the woman. "Maybe call her Patient One, something like that. But I'd want to see what she went through and how that was different from the procedures that are being used now." Ramona looked at the older woman who had willingly married herself to her work, clearly feeling that the institute was doing something extraordinarily good. Judging by the way Wilma's face relaxed, she'd found the right angle, Ramona thought.

"I just want to immerse myself in the institute's history. If I'm to do the Armstrong institute any good, I have to know everything about it first," she explained.

Wilma said nothing for a moment, then slowly nodded. "I suppose you have a point." She opened her middle drawer and took something out. She held out a plastic card. "I have an access card."

Though she wanted to snatch it, Ramona restrained her impulse. Her hand remained at her side. "That's good to know."

Wilma looked at her, confused. "You don't want the card?"

More than you could possibly know. Out loud, she continued with her charade. "Not at the moment. I need to get a list of questions together first so I don't wind up spending a weekend in there. But I'll gladly take you up on your kind offer when I'm ready."

Wilma put the card back in its place and shut the drawer. "Fair enough."

Ramona walked out of the clinic smiling to herself. This way, if the topic should come up, Paul's trusted receptionist could tell him that she'd been in no hurry to run off to the basement and go rifling through the archives.

Her plan was to wait until Friday, take Wilma's access card and then go down after everyone had left for the weekend. She wanted to go through the files at her leisure, without worrying that someone might walk in on her.

Ramona didn't bother to attempt to tamp down her excitement.

Hang on just a little bit longer, Mom. If there's someone out there with your DNA, I'll find them. I promise.

Paul glanced at his watch as he came to the end of the report he'd been working on. The same report he'd been struggling with for the past few days, that had kept him prisoner in his seat because he'd vowed he wasn't going to go home until he finished it, even if it *was* Friday night.

As if Friday nights were different from any other night, he mocked himself. He'd long ago sacrificed any kind of social life to make sure that the institute remained on the cutting edge of its field.

This meant at times having to wade through myriad rules and regulations. It was enough to make a man permanently cross-eyed.

He made a few notations, then sat back in his chair

and sighed. Well, the report was finally finished. It wasn't an outstanding piece of work, but it was finished.

Wanting to go, Paul forced himself to quickly reread the document.

Which was a good thing because on the third page, he came to a glaring empty space. That was when he remembered that he'd deliberately left the blank area to remind himself that he needed a particular set of statistics to hammer home his point. A set of statistics that weren't readily accessible because it had been bundled up with a large set of "precomputer" data and deposited in the room where they kept the rest of the files and folders that had not been input or scanned into the database.

Paul blew out a breath. He was tired and hungry. Monday was soon enough for him to go down there and retrieve the information.

No, he contradicted himself in the next moment. That would be putting things off, and he knew he'd spend the weekend being haunted by the omission until he finally came in on Monday morning and got the missing data he needed.

He might as well get it over with and do it tonight, Paul told himself. Otherwise, he was going to wind up sacrificing his weekend.

What weekend? he mocked himself. The only thing that made the following two days different from the five he'd just been through was that some of the time, he didn't come back into his office at the institute.

Well, if you did something about this attraction you're feeling for Ramona, maybe you'd finally have *a social life.*

Paul shook his head, pushing down his thoughts.

Opening his desk drawer, he took out the white plastic card he needed to gain access to the archives, picked up his briefcase and walked out of his office.

The lights in the building had been dimmed. It felt exceptionally lonely, he mused as he walked down the corridor to the elevator.

The sound of the car's arrival seemed amplified against the wall of silence. He got on and pressed the button for the basement.

Getting off the elevator, he turned right and made his way down the winding corridor. The lighting here was even dimmer than on the other floors. His destination had originally been used as a bank vault. When his father had bought the property for the institute, he'd had the existing building demolished, but he'd left the vault. Keeping it intact appealed to him for reasons the man never went into and no one—except his mother—even questioned that he'd seen fit to retain it.

When he reached the reinforced-steel door, he was about to slide his card through the slot when he saw that it wasn't necessary. The door was standing ajar.

The hairs on the back of his neck instantly rose. Who could be here at this hour? He debated calling 911, but decided to hold off in case it was one of the staff members who had access to the archives. He needed to check this out further.

Cautiously, Paul slipped in as silently as he could. Putting down his briefcase, he slowly crept toward the back of the vault where the files were actually kept. His father had taken an active part in designing the three-story building that was now the institute, and these plans had extended to renovating the vault, as well.

Gerald Armstrong had insisted that it not only have its own source of power, but a backup generator as well in case the city suffered another massive power failure like the one that had thrown the East Coast into darkness decades ago. In addition, he'd authorized that a very small powder room be added, as well. It was because of this last touch that the institute's "unique file room" had been the subject of more than one magazine article.

As he made his way in, Paul could have sworn he heard someone moving around in the center of the vault. Again he wondered who could be down here at this hour.

And then he had his answer.

There, directly in front of him, was Ramona Tate. She was taking pictures with what looked like the world's tiniest camera.

Paul was stunned. Was she spying on them? Collecting data for another fertility organization?

Even as the questions occurred to him, Paul felt anger bubbling up inside.

"What do you think you're doing, Ramona?" he demanded, coming forward.

Her nerves already pulled so taut that they were ready to break at any moment, Ramona's heart instantly flew into her throat. She screamed as she swung around. And then, when she saw that it was Paul, she breathed a sigh of relief.

Relief, however, was short-lived.

"I said, what do you think you're doing here?" he repeated. This time his voice was unnervingly cold and hard.

It took her a moment to collect herself. *Always go with the truth as your foundation.* Ramona sincerely believed that. It made for fewer mistakes in the long run.

She looked at him as if to silently say that was self-explanatory. "I'm just going through the files in the archives."

"You're photographing them," he pointed out angrily. "Why?"

She had an answer prepared for that, too. "So I don't have to come back again. This way, I can read through them upstairs instead of in this tiny, cramped space."

Because weakness of any kind embarrassed her, she didn't add that she was a claustrophobic. While closed-in places did not cause her to assume a fetal position, the sooner she was out of here, the better. That was one of the reasons she'd left the door open. She wanted to feel air coming in even though, logically, that was impossible, given her position.

"But *why* are you going through the files in the archives?" These were mostly patient folders and trials that belonged to his father. He didn't know what was in each file, but his protective instincts definitely kicked in. He might have never been close to the man, but he didn't want to see his father's name dragged through the mud, either.

"I'm preparing a piece on the institute—" She stopped and looked at him, slightly puzzled. "I must have told you that. Anyway, I just need a little history for background information. You know, how your father didn't give up despite X amount of false starts and near misses."

Paul picked up one of the folders she'd just been photographing and read the label across it. "You're in the patient files."

"It's a personal story," she replied, unfazed. "Don't worry, I'll change the names to protect the parties involved."

But Paul shook his head as he replaced the folder. "No, you won't."

Did he think she was that careless? "Yes, I will," she insisted.

"No, you won't, because you're not going to go through any more of the files," he told her firmly. "And you're not going to use the information from the ones you already photographed."

She still hadn't found her mother's file, but she knew it had to be here somewhere. She'd been down here for the past two hours and felt that she was getting close. All she needed was a few more minutes to find it. But he wasn't going to give her those minutes, she knew, looking at the set of Armstrong's jaw. She was going to have to come back later and it would undoubtedly be harder for her to get in. That really frustrated her.

"Why?" It was her turn to challenge him. "What are you afraid I'm going to find here?" The moment the words were out of her mouth, she realized that she'd pressed his buttons. Obviously he didn't like having his orders questioned.

"I think that's about enough. I want you to leave now. We'll discuss this on Monday." The tone he used promised that there would be no discussion, only a lecture. And he'd be the one giving it.

There was no point in arguing with him. He wasn't about to give in. She was just going to have to find an excuse to get back here and find her mother's file. She didn't care what it took.

For now, Ramona gave him a small salute. "You're the boss, Doctor," she told him.

He thought he detected a hint of mockery in her voice. "Yes, I am," he answered curtly.

She began to walk away. He was right behind her. Did he think she was going to make a mad dash back? "Are you planning on following me?" she wanted to know.

He was tired. He could definitely come back for the

statistics he needed on Monday. The report he'd worked on wasn't about to go anywhere over the weekend.

"Yes, I am."

She turned to look at him over her shoulder as she continued walking. "I'm not cattle that you have to herd."

"Never said you were." He pointed toward the door that was still standing ajar. "Now, just go." It was an order.

She didn't care for his tone. Still looking over her shoulder, she was about to tell him just that when she tripped over the briefcase he'd dropped. Thrown off balance, Ramona stumbled and pitched forward. Not wanting to smash her head against the concrete floor, Ramona grabbed the first thing she could to steady herself. The last thing in the world she wanted was to fall flat on her face in front of him.

Unfortunately, the first thing she managed to grab was the steel handle on the vault door. She yanked it toward her. The next moment, she heard an awful clicking sound. Her stomach seized up as she realized what she'd done. Praying she was wrong, she tried the door. And paled when she found it wouldn't budge.

"What are you waiting for? Go ahead," Paul ordered. He'd almost grabbed her himself when she was falling and was glad he was spared. He was fairly certain that it would have been the beginning of a huge mistake.

"I can't," she told him through gritted teeth.

He was in no mood for games. She was looking particularly gorgeous tonight, but she was becoming damn irritating. "Listen—"

"You said that when the building was constructed, this vault was left intact. Did anyone consider using it for a panic room?"

What an odd question. And one that could be asked far better outside this enclosed area than in. "Not that I know of, why?"

She sucked in air before answering. Was it her imagination, or was she choking? There was distress in her eyes as she turned around to look at him. "The door's locked."

His eyes narrowed. She had to be pulling his leg. He hadn't thought that her sense of humor would be on this low a level. "What do you mean 'locked'?"

"As in 'won't open.' As in 'trapped.'" Did he really need any more synonyms? "I—accidentally pulled it shut when I tripped."

She was putting him on to see his reaction, Paul thought. "No, you didn't."

"Fine." She stepped to the side and gestured toward the steel door. "Have it your way. *You* open it. I really hope you can," she added.

But he couldn't.

Chapter Eleven

Paul had hoped against hope that Ramona was mistaken—that she hadn't pulled the door shut all the way when she'd grabbed it. But one fruitless tug told him she had.

He turned away from the immobile steel and looked at her. "It's locked."

"That's what I said," Ramona retorted, her voice quavering. With effort she desperately tried to keep her voice from cracking. Panic was waiting just beyond the perimeter to grip her in its bony fingers.

Damn it, he'd been meaning to put in safeguards against this very thing happening, but it was one of those nonpressing things he felt comfortable about putting off. He was far from comfortable now.

Searching for a way out, he found none. "I don't think you understand what I'm saying," he told Ramona.

"It's locked. I got it," she said sharply. "I told you."

Ramona took in a shaky breath. She needed to calm down. But confined places made her think of graves. It was only because she was so desperate to get the information she needed for her mother—and to secure the information that would give credence to the rumors that her editor had her investigating—that she'd even stepped into the tomblike room.

She looked at Paul hopefully. "But you can override it, right?"

"Override it?" Paul repeated. What did she think he was, a magician?

"Yes, as in making it open up again. You know, with a code or a master card or something like that." She was beginning to sound like a babbling loon, she chided. With effort, she got hold of herself. "You're the chief of staff," she argued when he continued looking at her as if he was still waiting for her to make sense. "You're supposed to have some kind of extra power over the rest of us."

"I must have missed that in the manual," he quipped. "No 'extra powers' to speak of."

Oh, please let him be kidding. "Then you can't open it?"

"It's a converted bank vault," he needlessly pointed out.

"I know what it is." She banked down the hysteria that was beginning to enter her voice. "But I still thought—"

"That means," he continued as if she hadn't spoken, "it's on a timer."

A timer. A timer meant that it was set to a specific hour. Like every hour on the hour or something like that. She could handle an hour. Maybe. "So when does it open again?"

He glanced at his watch. There were times when he forgot not only the time, but the day. His watch had both. "It's Friday."

"Yes. So?" she prodded, waiting for him to tell her something she could cling to.

Paul realized that he was going to be stuck with this woman for an entire two days and three nights. He met the prospect with conflicted feelings. Some he understood and others he didn't want to understand. They were far too personal, far too stirring. They had no place here.

"The vault opens again at 8:00 a.m. on Monday morning."

"Monday morning?" It was all Ramona could do to keep from screaming out the words. "You're kidding, right?"

"Unless someone comes and overrides the timer from the outside, no, I'm not kidding," Paul told her. "The door won't open until Monday."

"But we can't stay here that long."

Although he liked the idea of being alone with this woman, having her trapped in order to do it was definitely not what he would have had in mind. "I don't think there's much choice."

For a moment, desperation reduced her thought process to nothing, freezing it in place as panic encroached upon her. Focusing every fiber within her, she willed herself to calm down. Once she did, she remembered. She had her cell phone with her.

"There's always a choice, Doctor," she retorted happily. Flipping her phone open, she tapped out 911, only to get nothing. She tried again before she looked at the tiny illuminated screen. "There're no signal bars," she noted numbly. "There're always supposed to be bars." She looked up from her phone to Armstrong's face. "They promised bars," she lamented, referring to the commercials about her service provider. "Why aren't there bars?"

"That's probably because they never tried to use their phones in an underground vault."

She wasn't going to accept defeat. She couldn't. "Do you have your cell phone on you?"

He always kept it in his pocket. "Yes, but the result will be the same," he warned her.

Maybe he was wrong. Maybe there was something wrong with her phone. She didn't care what the reason was, she just wanted a signal.

"Try it," she ordered. She was no longer an employee trying to curry his favor—she was just a woman on the verge of a breakdown for a completely embarrassing reason and she knew it—which made it all the worse to bear.

Rather than argue, Paul took out his phone and tapped out the three numbers. "Nothing," he declared in response to the quizzical look in her eyes.

She could feel the panic in her chest. "You seem awfully calm for someone locked in a vault until Monday morning," she accused.

Maybe he was doing this to teach her a lesson for snooping where he didn't want her to, she thought. Ramona grasped on to the slim sliver of hope, praying she was right.

"Panicking isn't going to help us any," he pointed out.

She still didn't want to give up. "Isn't there some way to signal someone?" she wanted to know. "What about the security guards?"

Paul reviewed the men's responsibilities in his mind. "There're video cameras throughout the building. They monitor them in the security room." The room was off to the side of the building.

Oh, thank God. "Well, there you go," Ramona said, relief coating every syllable. "They'll come down when they see us."

"*If* they see us," Paul corrected. "There's no camera in here. Hardly anyone ever comes down to look through the archives," he pointed out.

Ramona could almost feel her heart sinking in her chest. She looked around the room as if the walls literally *were* starting to close in on her. Thoughts of suffocation began to crowd her head. "How much air do we have?"

"That's no problem," Paul was quick to assure her. "The original designer made sure there'd be plenty of air circulating through here so that whatever people had in their safe-deposit boxes wouldn't eventually dry out. My father maintained the system for the files he had stored here."

For a second, she closed her eyes and murmured, "Thank God." And then her eyes flew open as other, possibly insurmountable problems occurred to her. "What about other things?"

"Other things?" he repeated, not following her line of thinking.

"Food, water..." She didn't feel like getting personal right now, but there was no way around it. "Bathroom facilities," she concluded uncomfortably.

"There's a watercooler behind the last cabinet." He pointed to the right. "And for reasons I never understood, there's also a powder room located on the far side." He indicated the opposite wall. "As for food—" Well, there they struck out. "Nobody was ever supposed to be down here long enough to get hungry."

Two whole days without food. People didn't starve after two days, right? She tried to make the best of the situation. "Oh well, I've been meaning to go on a diet," she murmured. Her biggest problem wasn't food, it was keeping her thoughts under control and not panicking.

Paul's eyebrows drew together as he looked at her. "Why would you want to do that?"

"Because I'm overweight." According to her scale, she was three pounds over her ideal weight. She'd been meaning to cut back a little. She just hadn't thought about doing it while locked in a safe.

When she looked at Armstrong, he made no secret of the fact that he was still scrutinizing her. "No, you're not."

In the midst of her mounting panic, Ramona paused to look at the chief of staff in surprise. She wouldn't have thought that he'd even notice something like that. She realized that in his own unassuming way, he'd just given her a compliment—while sealed inside a vault.

"Thank you," she murmured.

There was air, there was air—he'd told her so and he wasn't the kind of man to lie, she tried to console herself. So why did she feel as if she was suffocating? Was it just her mind playing tricks on her?

"Won't someone wonder where you are?" she asked hopefully.

It was Friday evening. Everyone he knew had plans. Plans that didn't include him. His time was usually spent working or making plans for the coming week's work. This weekend, like most, he was going to spend by himself.

"No," he told her quietly. And then he looked at her as the same thought occurred to him. Just because he wasn't panicking didn't mean he wanted to be here until Monday morning. "How about you? Someone's going to miss you if you don't show up tonight or tomorrow morning, am I correct?"

Since she had such a sporadic work schedule, she knew her mother would just assume she was working. Katherine Tate wouldn't dream of interrupting her when she was working, so there wouldn't even be an attempt to call her.

Not that that would lead to anything anyway, she thought, looking at the nonreceptive cell phone in her hand.

She shoved the phone angrily into her pocket. "No," she answered, "I don't."

"I find that impossible to believe."

Ramona looked at him. Armstrong wasn't being sarcastic, he was serious. She repressed her fraying temper.

"You have no idea how much I wish you were right. But you're not." Her voice sounded ragged to her own ears as she asked him, "What are we going to do?"

Paul studied her for a moment. It wasn't his imagination. There were now beads of perspiration forming along her hairline. It still wasn't hot enough in here for that sort of reaction.

"Are you all right?" he asked. "You look a little—" Paul searched for the right word. "Spooked," he finally said. "Definitely agitated."

"I'm fine," she retorted. This was not the time to

reveal a weakness. She didn't want to have the fact that she had claustrophobia getting around.

But it seemed to be too late. "No, you're not," he countered. And then he realized what he was seeing. "You're claustrophobic, aren't you?"

"No," she snapped. And then she drew in a lungful of air. What was the point of denying it? He was going to find out soon anyway. She didn't know how much longer she could maintain this facade. "Yes. Yes, I'm claustrophobic," she retorted.

It didn't make sense. "But I've seen you in elevators."

Yoga and a few other crutches had taught her how to cope within a situation for a limited amount of time. "I can usually keep it under wraps as long as the confinement is for a short period of time." She glanced around the room again like a caged animal. "Not eternity."

"Unless you're a fruit fly, Monday morning is hardly an eternity away," he told her, hoping that putting things into perspective would help her cope.

Ramona made no answer. Instead, she looked down at her palms, which were growing progressively sweatier. She rubbed one hand against the other in an attempt to dry them off. The sweatiness continued.

He was a doctor, Paul reminded himself. His first obligation was to his patient and while Ramona was not his patient, in the typical sense of the word, it took no stretch of the imagination to see that Ramona Tate was sorely in need of a physician to help her cope with the predicament they found themselves in.

"The first thing we need to do," he told her, taking her hand and leading her away from the steel door, "is get your mind off the situation."

Was he delusional? "We're *in* the situation," she reminded him sharply. "In a small, steel-walled, 'situation' that could at any minute suffocate us. Snuff us out just like that."

"Not unless the air stops being pumped in," he pointed out.

She looked up to the air vents. "There's a thought." Her throat tightened in fear.

"There's a backup generator in case this one fails," he told her.

She searched his face. His eyes were kind. She shook her head. "You're just saying that to make me feel better."

"Yes," Paul admitted. "I would. But luckily, I don't have to. My father left nothing to chance," he assured her. "The basement is hooked up to the system that runs through the rest of the institute. There are backup generators in case of a major power failure. Don't forget, we have donor eggs and sperm stored here. We can't afford to have the refrigeration system break down, even for a small amount of time. If we actually lost power, any stored embryos we have would be destroyed in a matter of hours. Even a short amount of time would likely have an adverse effect."

All right, so there was air. That still didn't keep the

walls from feeling as if they were closing in on her, but at least she'd die breathing.

She slowly took in a breath and then released it just as slowly in an attempt to calm her erratic pulse.

"Better?" Paul asked her gently. He was still holding her hand.

He was trying to be nice, she thought, feeling somewhat guilty for what she'd been up to. She knew she couldn't blame him for this situation since it was really her fault they were locked in. The fact that he wasn't blaming her said a great deal about his character. Paul Armstrong was a really decent man, she decided.

"Better," she acknowledged in a quiet voice.

She was lying, Paul judged. The beads of sweat were still there, dampening her bangs. But at least she wasn't breaking down yet. Maybe he could still divert her attention, get her mind on something else.

There was an old sofa, a castoff from one of the consultation rooms, pushed up against one of the walls. It had been placed here rather than thrown out so that when someone did come down to the archives, they could go through the files and read whatever they needed in comfort. He led her over to it now.

"Why don't you sit down here and talk to me," he encouraged.

She stared at him blankly. Was he going to interrogate her? Did he suspect what she was actually doing down here? "About?"

As he sat down, he lightly tugged on her hand, silently urging her to take a seat, as well. "Anything you want."

Ramona sat down. She licked her lips, thinking about the fact that she'd skipped lunch today and her stomach was reminding her that it felt damn empty.

"How do we get out of here?"

"Monday morning, the time lock will be released," he told her patiently. She looked away. He saw the building panic in her face. "Look at me, Ramona. Look at me," he repeated more firmly but still kind. When she did, he continued, his voice reassuring, patient. "It's going to be all right. Fear is just a trick our minds play on us. This is a big room, just a big room, nothing more. Not a tomb," he said, looking into her eyes. "A room."

"Are you sure there's no way to get someone down here?"

"I'm sure. Everyone but the security guards is gone. We had an emergency earlier, but we managed to stabilize the woman enough to transport her and her husband to the hospital. She's resting comfortably now and, more important to her, she's still pregnant," he added.

He had a nice smile, she thought. Why hadn't she noticed that before? "You really are into this, aren't you?"

She had a way of hopping around from topic to topic. He wasn't sure what she was referring to. "Into what?"

"Making couples into parents."

"Yes."

She tried desperately to concentrate on the conversation. "Why?"

"Because I know that the people who come here to the institute, ready to give us their last penny, to borrow more if need be, just for the privilege of having a baby, will make wonderful parents. Because that's what being a good parent is all about. Sacrifice. Putting the child in front of your own needs. If it's in my power to help them, it would be unconscionable for me not to."

She nodded. "It must make you feel a little like God, doing that. Creating life."

"I'm not the one 'creating it,'" he protested. "And I certainly don't feel like God. If you want to follow the creation route, I'm just an instrument in all this. If God doesn't want it to happen, then nothing I do will make it so."

Ramona was quiet for a moment, reading between the lines. "So you've had failures."

He thought of the looks on the women's faces when he had to tell them that the procedure hadn't resulted in a pregnancy. Thought of the way his sister Olivia looked when she came into his office a couple of weeks ago, desperate. Each time he lost a battle, it took a piece out of him. "Sadly, yes."

She prodded a little further. "Then not every embryo takes?"

"No." He really wished it would. Each failure, to him, represented a child who would never be born. "That's a matter of record," he told her. His eyes held hers for a long moment. "Was that what you were looking for? The failures?"

The question had come out of nowhere and in her present state, she wasn't as prepared to answer as she should have been. She almost stuttered as she made the denial. "No, I told you, I'm doing a piece on the institute's history and—"

He cut her short. "I know what you told me." Paul moved in closer to her. "Now, I'm interested in the truth."

"I *am* telling you the truth," she protested, doing her best to sound indignant. She couldn't quite carry it off.

"All right," he allowed patiently, "then tell me the *whole* truth."

Maybe it was the claustrophobia kicking up another notch and stealing oxygen from her brain. For whatever reason, she felt she had to give him something more than she had. He was surprisingly too intuitive to be satisfied with her pat alibi.

He understood the bond between mothers and their children, she mused. Suddenly, she knew what piece of the truth to give him.

Taking a breath, and then another because the first didn't feel sufficient, Ramona began. "As it turns out, putting this in the 'truth is stranger than fiction' column, a couple of decades ago my mother donated her eggs to the institute."

He kept looking at her, wondering if she was fabricating this story on the spur of the moment. But a moment later, he decided that she looked too distressed to be making it up. Either that, or she was one hell of an actress. "And you're trying to find out if you have siblings?"

"Not exactly," she corrected. "I'm trying to save my mother's life."

Chapter Twelve

Paul's eyes met hers. On the scale of one to ten for dramatic statements, the one she'd just uttered was a ten. If she meant to capture his attention, she'd succeeded.

"I'm listening."

Ramona suppressed any last-minute doubts. What did she have to lose? He couldn't take her to task for being concerned about her mother, he wasn't the type. And if she gave him this, it might make him stop looking for other reasons why she'd ventured down here, quite apparently far out of her comfort zone.

Maybe he'd even help her find the file.

"My mother has leukemia. And it's progressing." She paused a beat to keep her voice from quavering.

"The doctor said she's going to die without a bone-marrow transplant." Ramona bit her lower lip. The pain in her voice was something she didn't have to fake. She experienced it with every word. "Mine's not a match. She has no brothers or sisters. Neither do I. At least, none that I knew about—" She took a breath. "And then I remembered."

"Remembered what?"

She told him just the way it happened. "That when I was a teenager, I stumbled across an old box of receipts and what looked like bills in the back of my mother's closet—I was looking for a pair of her shoes I wanted to borrow," she explained in case he was going to ask why she was rummaging through her mother's things. "Mixed in was a medical statement for a donation she'd made years ago. She donated her eggs to the institute." Her eyes were on his now. "I need to know if they were even used and if so, by whom and whether the implantation resulted in a viable birth."

There was silence for a moment, and then he shook his head. Ramona wondered if she'd set herself up for a fall. Had she been wrong about him after all? Was he strictly by the numbers with no heart?

"Why didn't you just tell me what you were looking for?"

"Because I had no idea what your reaction would be," she said honestly.

"Under the circumstances, did you really think I'd say no?"

"I didn't know you. If I asked and you said no, you might have decided to put safeguards in to prevent my looking. This was too important to take a chance on that. My mother's life depends on it."

She wasn't aware that she was crying until she saw Paul reach into his pocket and take out a handkerchief. Very gently, he took her chin in his hand and wiped away the tears that were sliding down her cheeks.

The movement was so delicate, so kind, Ramona could feel her heart swelling in her chest. None of her safeguards were in place.

Her eyes met his and their gazes held for what felt like eternity.

Again, she stopped breathing, but this time her fear of small, enclosed places had nothing to do with her response. Or with the sudden increased beating of her heart.

Without realizing she was doing it, Ramona silently willed him to kiss her. If she kissed him first, it would throw everything off. She didn't want seduction— because it would be seen as that—to be perceived as part of her arsenal in going after the evidence to substantiate her story and, in hindsight, that would be what Paul would think.

But if he kissed her, well, these things happened sometimes, especially under the unusual circumstances that they found themselves in.

The fact that she was willing him to kiss her had nothing to do with her ultimate goals was something she wasn't going to think about now.

* * *

Paul knew he shouldn't.

He was a grown man with better-than-average self-control. He always had been.

And maybe that was the problem. He'd used it so often, held himself in check in so many different ways—be it denial of his own desires, or simply holding his temper in check when it came to dealing with Derek—that something felt as if it was cracking inside him now. He wanted—*needed*—to break free. To act on these feelings and unexplored emotions that were rushing over him now.

Maybe it was the look in her eyes that finally pushed him over the edge. He really wasn't sure.

The pure, basic fact of the matter was that he slipped his fingers into her hair, framed her face with his hands and brought his mouth down on hers slowly enough for her to pull away if she so chose.

But she didn't pull away.

Instead, she offered herself up to what was happening, making the kiss between them flower into something far more powerful than what it was intended to be. It wasn't a kiss to console, or comfort, or support. Rather, it was something so powerful that it overwhelmed both of them.

Paul felt his control shatter and Ramona's lips met his own. Suddenly, passion and desire were all around him, urging him on, making him realize that he wanted her. Not just to hold, not just to kiss, but to have. He wanted to make love with her.

The last time he'd made love with a woman seemed light-years away; he couldn't even summon up a face, a name. Hell, right now, he realized, as fire raced through his veins, he'd have trouble summoning up his *own* name.

There was nothing and no one, only this woman whose very presence was sending him into an emotional tailspin. And that unnerved him.

Badly.

This was better, better than she'd even imagined. The taste of his lips excited her to the point that it took supreme effort not to begin tearing at his clothes. She couldn't return his passionate kisses, couldn't get caught up in the fever pitch that seemed to be sizzling between them. Because he would think she'd planned it all. And he'd hate her even more than he would once he found out who she really was.

The thought chilled her for a moment, but then her need to be with this man, to feel his hands on her, to have him come to the ultimate union with her, over-whelmed everything else. All she had was the moment and she meant to savor it for the thrill that it was. Later would have to take care of itself. She wanted Now.

A moment ago—or maybe a lifetime ago—they'd been sitting sedately next to each other on the sofa. Now their bodies were pressed against one another. The instant she felt his hands, pulling her blouse from her waistband, her fingers began to tug at his shirt, all but ripping away buttons as she yanked them through the buttonholes.

She could feel her breath growing shorter, but this time it wasn't because of any sort of panic. This time it was because of anticipation. Anticipation that blazed through her body like a wildfire as they discarded their clothes in a growing frenzy.

Paul couldn't believe this was happening, that he was really *so* immersed in this woman whose soulful eyes had gotten through his carefully constructed reserve.

But he had to regain at least a modest amount of control over himself, he thought fiercely. Though he felt the heat of her response, he had to be sure that he wasn't just forcing himself on her because her claustrophobia had rendered her defenseless. He wanted their joining to be mutual.

She was beneath him on the sofa, the movement of her body setting him ablaze. But he had to give her a chance to back out. So, with extreme effort, Paul pulled himself back just far enough to give her room to slip out from under him, and looked down into her face.

She was breathless, but it didn't bother her. She was that wrapped up in what was happening, that wrapped up in these extreme, delicious sensations that were holding her in their grip. And suddenly, the building crescendo halted like a video on pause.

She felt air along her skin as he created a space. Was he getting up? Now?

"Is something wrong?" she asked in a voice that was hardly above a whisper.

As she spoke, her breath trailed along his skin, tightening his groin. He wanted her with such an intensity that he almost broke.

"Wrong?" he echoed. "It's never felt this right," he confessed, even as he counseled himself to dole out his words sparingly.

She didn't understand. Her body was all but screaming for his. "Then why did you stop?"

He watched her lips move. It took everything he had not to press his against them. "Because I want to make sure you don't want to change your mind."

"We're taking a vote?" she asked incredulously.

The next moment, she heard him laugh, the sound rumbling along her abdomen and breasts, teasing her almost to the breaking point. Her core was moistening, aching to accept him. She didn't bother with words. Instead, she framed his face with her hands and brought his mouth down to hers.

Bathed in kisses that Paul pressed along her neck and shoulders, Ramona felt she was more than ready for him when Paul finally locked his fingers with hers and slowly entered her body.

Ramona gasped as the first forceful wave of a climax exploded through her. She began to move her hips frantically in order to reach the next plateau.

And then the next one.

By the time they reached the ultimate limit, they were both drenched, breathless and almost beyond exhaustion, but content.

She felt herself falling back to earth after what amounted to a surreal experience. Paul Armstrong was easily the very best lover that she had ever had. He had surprised her with his technique, his gentleness and his prowess. Ramona kept her arms wrapped around him. She was holding on so tightly that she didn't think she was ever going to release him.

And part of her didn't want to.

She didn't want this moment to pass. She didn't want the world, with its myriad complications, to descend on her, robbing her of this wondrous sensation.

But all too soon he was rolling off her, sitting against the arm of the sofa, leaving open space next to her. Ramona doubted very much that this was just a random choice on his part. He knew, she thought, knew that the other way would make her feel hemmed in and stir up her claustrophobia all over again now that the temperature of her blood was returning to normal.

As he looked at Ramona, Paul searched his brain, trying to find something reassuring to say. Something that would let her know that this wasn't the way he ordinarily behaved, even under these extraordinary conditions.

He wanted to apologize—but he was only sorry if she felt compromised in any way. Because, looking at it from his own point of view, he was as far from sorry as a man could possibly be.

But how could he express any of that without

sounding as if this had all somehow been carefully plotted out and rehearsed?

Paul began haltingly, clearing his throat. He got no further than whispering her name. "Ramona…"

Ramona pressed her index finger to his lips, silencing him. For some reason, she had a feeling she knew what he was about to say and she didn't want him to agonize over what had just transpired.

"I know," she murmured.

And she did. She'd found out everything she needed to know about what had just happened between them just by looking at him. It was there in his eyes. And it was enough for her.

He looked at her quizzically. "You do?"

Touching his cheek, she smiled at him. He could almost feel that smile radiating warmth within his chest. "Yes."

Was the woman a witch, or just good at second-guessing? He had to ask. "And what is it you think you know?"

Funny, she never thought of herself as being particularly insightful when it came to men, at least not on a personal level. When it came to breaking news, she could read them like a book. This was different. It was as if, having made love with him, they were connected on a deeper level.

"That you didn't plan this. That you don't generally do this kind of thing and that you want me to know that you weren't trying to take advantage of me."

Paul stared at her for a long moment. It stretched out so far that she thought she'd really overstepped the line this time. Maybe she'd gotten it wrong after all. Maybe he had just fooled her.

No, she silently insisted. He wasn't that kind of person. She had to be right about him.

And then he said, "When you filled out your résumé, under special skills, why didn't you put down mind reading?"

Yes, she was right after all. Pleased, Ramona grinned. Grinned from ear to ear before answering his question. "I didn't want to brag."

"I see."

Propping himself up on his elbow, he lightly swept her hair from her face. There was a feeling going through him. He couldn't really begin to describe it. The closest he could come to it was admitting to himself that he felt happy. Lighter than air and really, really happy. He'd never felt that way before.

"It would have been nice to be forewarned, though. I wouldn't have bothered talking as much as I did. You could have just read my thoughts."

She laughed then, shaking her head. "You consider what you did a lot of talking?"

"For me."

"I see."

Just looking at him, all she wanted to do was kiss him again. And again. And then follow that to its natural conclusion one more time. Maybe two.

Giving in to her impulse, Ramona bent her head and pressed a kiss just above his collarbone. The small, guarded sigh that escaped his lips as she did so thrilled her and fueled her inclination to repeat at least part of what had just gone before.

Pressing him back against the sofa, she shifted so that this time she had the upper position. It wasn't about first moves anymore. It was about enjoying each other while the rest of the world was still at bay.

Ramona wreathed his face and neck with a string of fleeting, light kisses that she dispensed with growing fervor.

As spent as he thought he was, Paul had no choice but to rise up and offer her a return on her investment.

They made love again and then again after a sufficient amount of time had passed, turning the small confined former vault into a miniparadise where each had found his soul mate, as temporary as that might turn out to be.

And during all this time, the one constant that remained was that Ramona forgot about her fears.

All she felt was wondrously alive.

Because of him.

Ramona hung on to that for as long as she could. And, without being aware of when and how it actually happened, she dozed off in his arms.

Chapter Thirteen

"Breakfast," Paul announced the next morning, his voice cutting through the last layer of sleep swirling in her brain.

Ramona blinked several times to focus. Somehow, Paul had managed to get up without waking her. He'd had to be part contortionist to have managed that feat.

He'd gotten dressed as well, putting on everything except his white lab coat. That, she now realized, he'd draped over her to give her some semblance of privacy.

Again, she was caught off guard by his thoughtfulness. There was so much more to the man than she'd originally thought.

Sitting up, holding his lab coat pressed against her,

Ramona looked at the energy bars that were in the palm of his hand. She couldn't remember anything ever looking so good to her. Controlling the impulse to grab them as her stomach all but moaned in its emptiness, she looked up at his face instead.

"Where did you get those?"

He nodded toward the worn, black leather object that had tripped her and set off this chain of events last night. "I forgot I had them in my briefcase."

"Anything else in your briefcase, like coffee? Or a shower?" she asked longingly. She could use both—and a toothbrush, she thought, running her tongue over her teeth.

Paul smiled and shook his head. "Sorry, just these two energy bars."

"Don't be sorry," she told him. And then a thought hit her. "Unless you're not planning on sharing them with me."

"Actually, you can have them both." Paul deposited the energy bars next to her on the sofa. "I'm really not hungry."

The hell he wasn't, she thought. He was just making that up so that she wouldn't feel guilty eating both bars. She might be incredibly hungry, but she still had a conscience.

"Oh, don't get all heroic on me. How can you not be hungry?" she wanted to know. "If you don't have something, you're going to start nibbling on the first thing you find—like me."

His smile widened. "Not completely without merit."

The bars were identical. Raspberry flavored with chocolate drizzled over them. She picked up the one closest to her. "I bet you say that to all the girls you fool around with in the vault."

The very memory made him smile more broadly. It took effort not to pick up where they had left off last night. "That would be a minuscule number—as in one."

Ramona smiled at that, and, as he'd already noted more than once, her smile seemed to light up the entire area.

She looked down at the lab coat. "I think I'd better get dressed before I start in on this little feast," she quipped, nodding at the energy bar.

"Right."

Before she could ask, Paul turned his back to her, allowing her a little privacy, even though what he *really* wanted to do was tell her that she didn't need to get dressed again. Just looking at her stirred up other hungers. He tried to think of other things.

And remembered. "You said something last night about looking to see if you had any siblings."

"Yes," she answered guardedly.

"You realize that means invading the privacy of former patients."

For a second, she stopped tugging on her blouse. She knew all about those ramifications, but her cause was too precious, too important to let those concerns make her back off.

Was Paul going to stand in her way after all? "Yes," she replied haltingly, watching his back.

"You're going to have to proceed very cautiously," Paul warned her. "Otherwise, you're going to be leaving yourself—and the institute—open to a lot of legal red tape, not to mention the possibility of being sued by former patients if you wind up approaching them."

She released the breath she was holding. He wasn't telling her not to do it, he was telling her to be careful.

"I understand." Gratitude mingled with relief all through her. "You can turn around now," she told him. "I'm dressed."

More's the pity. Paul's expression never gave him away as he faced her again. "All right then, let's get to it," he said.

She was left to wonder what "it" was for only the briefest of seconds. Paul crossed back to the files and she realized that he was going to help her look. Energy bar in her hand, she scrambled to her feet.

Guilt almost got the better of her. Guilt because she hadn't been completely honest with him about her intentions.

The photographs she'd been taking weren't meant to be used as background material for a feature highlighting the positive side of the Armstrong Fertility Institute's history the way she'd told him. They were to cast light on its dark side. On the practice of substituting viable eggs and sperm for the ones that would never successfully produce a healthy child.

"I need to know the name your mother used when she made her donation," Paul was saying to her as she joined him. "Plus the year the procedure was done and, if possible, the name of any doctor she might have had contact with at the institute." He looked at the boxes of files before him. "The information we're looking for could be filed under any number of names," he told her.

Despite her inner turmoil, at the moment Ramona was busy savoring the taste of the energy bar she'd just unwrapped. It took a great deal of control not to wolf it down in three bites, but she managed to hold herself in check.

"There was no doctor's name on the statement," she told him. "And I don't recall the date, but I do remember the year." She gave it to him. "And I remember that my mother had used her maiden name, which struck me as odd at the time. It was Katherine Donnelly." She pressed her lips together. "Not much to go on, but—"

Ramona stopped midsentence. Was that a noise behind her? Her heart leaped. If she didn't know any better, she would have said it sounded as if someone was opening the vault door. But that was probably just wishful thinking on her part.

Even so, she crumpled up the empty wrapper and ran toward the steel door, bracing herself for disappointment. Paul, she realized, was right behind her.

"You heard it, too," she cried.

He had no time to answer.

The door *was* opening.

In less than a heartbeat, Ramona and he found themselves looking at Derek. It was hard, Paul thought, to say who looked more surprised, him or his twin. While beside him Ramona cried a relieved "Thank God," both he and his brother echoed the same question.

"What are you doing here?"

Derek, though, followed up his question with another one. His brother looked from him to Ramona and made no effort to hide a knowing grin. "Did I just interrupt something?"

It was Ramona who immediately answered. "Yes, suffocation."

On the heels of that, Paul explained, "We got locked in." But he saw that it wasn't enough. There was suspicion on his twin's face, that and an expression that bordered on a smirk. He knew the way Derek's mind worked. His twin was a womanizer and saw the world in those terms. "I came down to find some old files I wanted to check out for a report I was writing. Ramona is a great researcher, so I brought her with me to assist."

Maybe it was a good thing that there was no breeze down here, Ramona thought, because if there had been, it could have knocked her over just now. She only barely managed to keep her surprise from showing as she stopped short of contesting Paul's words.

The man was protecting her reputation. Somehow,

without knowing it, she'd managed to stumble across an old-fashioned knight in shining armor.

"And you?" Paul was asking his brother. "Why did you come down here?"

Instantly, another smile popped up. Derek's smile was all encompassing—and fake. Paul knew his twin far too well to be taken in by it. Still, he didn't bother to challenge his brother when Derek told him, "I just wanted to see how far back the files in the archives went. I was curious," he ended a bit lamely. "Keeping up with files wasn't exactly Dad's forte."

Paul let that slide, as well. He'd ask Derek more questions when they were alone. He owed his brother the courtesy of that rather than cornering him in front of someone outside the family.

Derek deftly turned the conversation back on them. "How did you get locked in?"

He was looking at Ramona when he asked the question, Paul noted.

"Long story," Paul answered. "Right now, all I want is a shower and a change of clothes. And something to eat that doesn't belong in the granola family."

"Ditto," Ramona chimed in with feeling. She was already turning on her heel to leave. Paul was quick to fall into step beside her.

Derek hung back as they walked out. He deliberately waited until his brother and Ramona had boarded the elevator and the doors had closed, separating him from them.

Satisfied that they were gone, Derek got down to business.

There were secrets down here in the old files, he thought, secrets that had to be worth something to someone. If he had a choice, he wouldn't do this, wouldn't go this far. But he had no choice. He was desperate enough to use anything at his disposal, whether it was ethical or not. Because, in the long run, it meant his life.

"We didn't get the information you were looking for," Paul said to her once the elevator doors opened on the first floor.

Getting off, Ramona was acutely aware of that fact. "I know." She couldn't have exactly gone rummaging around with his brother standing there. "I'll go back as soon as I can if you don't mind, but right now, I just want to assure myself that the sun is still in the sky and I can take in as much air as I want."

He smiled and reminded her, "You could in the vault, too."

Considering that the circumstances could have contributed to a complete breakdown on her part, she had a lot to be grateful to him for. "Logically, yes. But being claustrophobic doesn't have anything to do with logic. I really want to thank you for helping me get through that ordeal in one piece."

She saw him smile again and marveled at how the expression completely transformed him. Gone was the somber chief of staff. In his place was the young, sensually attractive man he somehow managed to keep hidden during the normal span of the day. The man who had made love with her last night, who had made her forget her fears.

"It was a dirty job," Paul responded, tongue in cheek, "but someone had to do it." And then he sobered slightly, as if the topic he was about to bring up deserved a display of decorum. "When do you want to come back to look for your mother's records?"

She glanced at her watch. It was a little after nine in the morning. "Would one o'clock be all right?"

It was Saturday. He had no firm plans for today. Spending time with her would definitely brighten it. "Fine. I can pick you up at your apartment if you like—"

She hadn't expected that. "You're coming, too?" Ramona didn't even try to hide her surprise. Why did he want to come with her? Was it because he still didn't trust her?

Paul nodded in answer to her question. "Two sets of eyes searching through the boxes will cut your time in half."

Relief briefly passed over her before guilt set in. He was being noble again. God, he was going to hate her once the other shoe dropped.

The thought weighed heavily on her. Far more heavily than when she thought she was trapped inside the vault and her claustrophobia had bordered on becoming unmanageable. She didn't want to seem un-grateful, but she really did want to be in the archives alone. She hadn't finished researching the topics she was being paid to flush out.

"Are you sure I'm not taking you away from something?"

"Very sure."

Paul resisted the impulse to slip his arm around her shoulders and pull her to him just for a moment. He didn't want to crowd her, but he had to admit to himself that there was something special about her. Something he wanted to explore. He'd never felt like this before about a woman. He wanted to see if it was the begin-ning of something wondrous, or if, like those old songs that littered musicals more than half a century ago, it was "just one of those things" that would eventually just fade away.

He wasn't a man anyone could ever accuse of being impulsive, but he allowed impulse to take over now. "Want to stop somewhere for a proper break-fast?" he asked her.

It was on the tip of Ramona's tongue to say no. The more she got involved with this man, the worse her lie of omission was going to seem to him. He was going to be furious with her and she was certain that there was nothing she could say that would convince him that she wasn't trying to use him.

Because, initially, she had.

He's going to think that no matter what, she silently

argued. She might as well enjoy what little time she had with him before the earthquake hit.

Nodding, she said, "Sounds good to me."

"Then let's go." He ushered her toward the front entrance. "I know this really great place that's open 24/7. Food just like mother used to make. At least," he amended as they stepped outside the doors, "your mother."

She looked at him. Bits and pieces were falling into place and he was becoming progressively more and more human to her. A good man who didn't deserve to be betrayed. "Didn't your mother cook?"

He laughed shortly. "I'm not sure my mother could find the kitchen with a compass. She's a Stanton," he told her. "Stantons, according to my mother, were born above menial things like cooking and other family-involved enterprises. They had a social standing to maintain, charity balls to throw and attend."

Ramona could feel her heart going out to him. What a lonely child he must have been. More than ever she was grateful for her mother—and more determined than ever to find the information that might save her life. "I am so sorry, Paul."

He believed her. He hadn't said it to make her pity him. Paul shrugged her sympathy away. "When you do without, you don't know what you're missing."

The same, he added silently, could be said about lovemaking. His previous experiences had convinced him that lovemaking and everything that went with it was way too overrated. Without emotion, sex for its own sake wasn't satisfying for him.

But he didn't feel that way anymore, not since Ramona had all but knocked his socks off last night.

He stopped by his parking space. Since it was Saturday, the lot was nearly empty. Ramona's vehicle was parked several yards away. "Do you want me to drive, or do you want to follow?"

She wouldn't have thought that Paul was sensitive to this extent. He was giving her a choice. Ordinarily, she would have said that a man like Paul was accustomed to making decisions and giving orders without regard for other people's feelings.

God, was she ever wrong about this man.

And maybe, just maybe, all these rumors that were flying around about the Armstrong Fertility Institute, his "baby," were just that. Rumors. Baseless rumors.

At least she could hope.

"I can appreciate the fact that you haven't written up your notes yet into any kind of final draft, but what, exactly, *do* you have?" Walter Jessup's voice crackled over her landline.

Ramona felt her heart sink in her chest. This wasn't a conversation she wanted to have now, but she knew she couldn't put her editor off. That was why she'd picked up the phone despite having caller ID and seeing his name on the LCD screen.

Big mistake.

After sharing a prolonged breakfast with Paul and discovering that the man she'd made soul-satisfying love with was a fascinating man in so many different ways, she'd all but floated home, humming off-key and grinning like some silly, love-struck schoolgirl.

Love-struck. Good word, she thought with amusement. Softer than being struck by lightning, but just as powerful.

What a difference a few hours had made in her world, she'd mused with a sigh as she'd unlocked the door to her apartment.

The plan had been to take a quick shower, change and meet Paul back at the institute, where he was going to help search for her mother's file.

Which meant that she couldn't do any other research, but that was okay with her. Her mother took precedence over that.

But she couldn't come out and say that to the man who was presently losing his temper on the other end of the line. The man whose call she shouldn't have taken.

Ramona tried to placate Jessup as best she could. For better or for worse, he was, after all, her boss. "I went through their old files—"

Jessup's mood instantly shifted. "Fantastic! Knew you'd come through. And what did you find out?"

She stifled a sigh and did her best to sound as positive as she could without giving him anything. "I'm not sure yet. I just took pictures of a number of the files. I haven't had a chance to go through any of them yet." She crossed her fingers that that would be the end of it for now.

It wasn't. "E-mail the files to me," Jessup instructed.

"But I just said I haven't read them yet." That wasn't entirely true, but she didn't want to hand the man anything he could actually use until she sorted it—and her own feelings—out. "It could all be nothing. I've just got a few rough notes to go with my research."

"I understand all that," Jessup barked impatiently. "I also understand that I sign your paychecks and I'd at least like to see some kind of return for the money that's been invested in this project. Now, e-mail those damn photographs to me. Do I make myself clear, Tate?"

"Yes, sir."

He had a perfect right to ask. He did, as he said, sign her paychecks. But that didn't stop her from putting conditions on her cooperation. She owed it to Paul, not because she'd slept with him, but because it was the decent thing to do. In her rush to find her mother's file and to earn as much money as she could to help defray her mother's medical expenses, she'd almost forgotten the meaning of that word. *Decent.* Her mother would have been heartbroken if she'd known.

"All right, Walter. But you have to promise to let me do the story my way. Don't give any of this information to some third-rate hack out to do a hatchet job on the institute just because he can."

She heard the editor pause for a long moment. The

silence worked its way into her nerves. And then she heard him grind out the words "All right."

Ramona wasn't convinced. "Your word, Walter. I want your word."

There was no indication of any emotion, good or bad, in Jessup's voice. He said, "You have my word," as if he was reading the words off a cue card.

"I'm holding you to that, Walter."

"Fine. And I'll be on the lookout for those photographs. Be sure you send them, Tate." The threat in his voice was barely veiled. The next moment, Jessup broke the connection.

Ramona hung up the phone and went to her desk.

She couldn't shake the feeling that she was making a mistake as she sat, holding the small, plug-in camera in her hand, waiting for her computer to power up. But there was little else she could do. She was going to have to send Jessup the files.

Chapter Fourteen

It was a little over a week later when Lisa burst into Paul's office like a petite hurricane. He looked up, silently wondering if a refresher course on doors, doorknobs and their function in the scheme of things might not be out of order.

Any mention of that topic instantly died as his sister, looking angrier than he could recall seeing her of late, demanded, "Have you seen it?"

A quick search of his memory banks came up empty. "I might be able to answer that question better if I knew what you're referring to, Lisa," he said, deliberately using a calm voice and hoping it might rub off on her.

He'd just been contemplating asking Ramona to spend the weekend at a bed-and-breakfast he'd come across this morning while doing a little research. Paul sincerely hoped that his sister's tirade wasn't going to take too long or interfere with his plans.

Lisa contemptuously tossed a magazine on his desk. Paul looked at it and read its name. He was not unfamiliar with the periodical. "The latest issue of *Keeping Up with Medicine.* I must have my copy here somewhere." Picking it up, he offered her back her copy.

Lisa made no effort to take the magazine. Her expression was stony. "Obviously, you haven't read the table of contents."

"I haven't had the chance." An uneasiness began to weave through him although he couldn't quite pinpoint the source. "Why? What's in it?"

"Look at page thirty." Lisa was seething as she bit off the words.

Paul dutifully turned to the page in question. He wasn't prepared for what he saw. His heart all but stopped as the title of the article jumped out at him: Armstrong Fertility Institute: Answer to a Prayer, or Beginning of a Nightmare?

He quickly skimmed the first paragraph in silence. The tone of the piece told him that the article was strictly focused on character assassination. In short order, he scanned the title page and the last paragraph. There was no byline. Credit for the article went to Anonymous.

He could understand Lisa's anger, but his was compounded. He didn't want to think what he was think-ing—but he couldn't help it.

Paul felt a fire burning a hole in his belly. Reining in his outrage, he looked up at his sister. His voice was low, dark. "Who wrote this?"

Lisa shrugged in frustration. "It doesn't say. I've already called the magazine, but they gave me the standard runaround. They 'can't reveal their sources,'" she told him. "Whoever this writer talked to knew a lot. They've got material in there that goes way back to when Dad was running this place." Lisa clenched her hands at her sides. "How did they *get* that kind of in-formation?" she demanded angrily.

And then her eyes widened.

Paul was oblivious to the light that had suddenly come into his sister's eyes. Neither did he notice the shift in demeanor as she mumbled, "I've got an idea. I'll get back to you on this."

Lisa left far more quietly than the way she'd entered. Paul was lost in his own thoughts, entertain-ing his own set of suspicions. Suspicions that caused him to be, in turn, angry, furious and incredibly dis-appointed. He tried to tell himself to reserve judg-ment, not to jump to any harsh conclusions until he talked to Ramona.

But everything pointed to Ramona being the culprit.

He had walked in on her in the vault taking photo-graphs of the files. Taking photographs, for God's sake.

All sorts of bells should have gone off when he saw

that. Industrial spies behaved that way, not company PR managers.

How obtuse could he have been?

Almost against his will, Paul followed his thinking to its logical conclusion—and he didn't like it.

Had everything been a lie? Had Ramona seen a way to use him, to placate him with her body so that he didn't ask her any more questions?

And that story about her mother, was it even real? Or was that just a product of her fertile imagination, created on the spur of the moment and fashioned out of something she'd noticed while going through the files?

He didn't want to believe it. But how could he *not* believe it? Sick at heart, he skimmed another two paragraphs in the article Lisa had brought to his attention.

This had Ramona's stamp all over it, he thought. Phrases jumped out at him. Phrases he'd heard her use.

Paul didn't want to dignify any of what he read in the article with a public denial, but he, Lisa and Derek were going to have to put their heads together and do some heavy-duty damage control here. The institute would suffer otherwise. For all he knew, it might already be too late. Coming on the heels of the formless rumors, this just might be a death blow.

He couldn't allow that.

Damage control. The thought struck him as ironic. Supposedly, that was what they had Ramona for, to implement damage control. But what they had actually done was to naively invite the fox into the henhouse.

He shook his head. Despite *everything,* he still wanted to believe Ramona wasn't responsible, that someone else was behind this. Someone with a vendetta against the institute or against his father or perhaps one of the three of them.

He was going to have no peace until he confronted Ramona with this article. No matter what the outcome, the sooner he got that over with, the better.

But first, he needed to check something out. Paul turned his chair to face his computer keyboard and began to type. Each strike of a letter cost him.

Ramona caught her lower lip between her teeth.

She reread the figures twice, then lifted the sheet on her desk to look at another spreadsheet that was just beneath it.

She wasn't wrong.

Wow. She hadn't even been looking for this when she started going through the files. The figures had caught her eye quite by accident.

There was a discrepancy.

A very large discrepancy.

No matter what she did, the tallies just didn't add up. Somehow, unaccounted for money was disappearing between spreadsheets. It wasn't obvious, but it was there, buried beneath invoices and laughable charitable write-offs. Laughable because a place like the Armstrong Fertility Institute didn't have charitable write-offs, it had A-list clients, some who came in through the front door, others who slipped in quietly via the "special" entrance, unwilling to let the public in on their private pain of infertility.

Here and there were Mr. and Mrs. Average American who had scraped together everything they had in order to obtain the one precious thing they *didn't* have: a baby. But none of the records, some of which went back over two decades, showed that any of the procedures were done pro bono. Everyone paid, some more handsomely than others, but everyone paid.

And yet, there were write-offs. How could that possibly be?

The word *embezzlement* popped up in her head in big, bold neon letters. It was a horrible thought, but it was the only explanation.

She had to tell Paul.

Derek might have been the one who hired her, but there was something about him that held her at bay, that didn't allow her to completely trust him. And as for Lisa, well, so far she hadn't gotten close to the woman, so the issue of trust hadn't been allowed to take root one way or the other.

But Paul was another matter. He'd gotten to her. Beneath his somber exterior was a kind, sensitive man who was also one hell of a lover. The corners of her mouth curved, remembering.

The doctor, bless him, was still trying to track down whoever had gotten her mother's eggs for her. The whole file was encoded to safeguard the recipient's identity, but Paul told her he was doing his best to get it deciphered. God knew he didn't have to go this extra mile for her, and yet he was. He understood what she was going through.

Which in turn made things very difficult for her.

Ramona sighed. She wanted to tell Paul what else she was up to, but she knew that the minute she made a clean breast of it, everything that had happened between them—that *was* happening between them—would be held suspect. And she would lose him.

And she couldn't even blame him.

Ramona drew in a ragged breath, wishing she'd never gotten involved in this investigation. But, in an odd way, if she hadn't, she would have never met the man who'd set her whole world on its ear and sent it spinning.

You can't miss what you never had.

Paul had told her that the evening when they'd gotten locked in the vault. And she knew that the converse was right, because if she ever lost him, she would be acutely aware of what she no longer had. Of what she'd lost. With all her heart she hoped she would never find out what that felt like.

And yet, how could she not? She just couldn't envision a happy ending to this.

Ramona heard the sharp rap on her door and hoped that whoever was standing on the other side would be quick about whatever they wanted. She wanted to talk to Paul as soon as possible.

She managed to successfully cover her impatience as she said, "Come in."

When she looked up and saw Paul walking in, her heart did a little dance in her chest. She wondered if she was ever going to be able to look at the man and not think of that night in the vault. It was almost as if she'd been born all over again that earthshaking night.

Paul was frowning.

It never occurred to Ramona that the frown was directed at her. She just thought that something had come up at work that displeased him.

Or maybe he had an inkling about what she'd just discovered. After all, he was an extremely intelligent man. Far more intelligent than she thought anyone gave him credit for because of his quiet demeanor.

Flashing a smile, she said, "I'm glad you're here, Paul. I was just about to come looking for you."

Yes, he just bet that she was. Undoubtedly to tell him another lie, or pump him for more information.

"Oh?"

There was something in his voice, something that didn't sound quite right, but she had no clue what it could be, so she plowed on.

"Yes, I found something you might be interested in." Ramona turned the spreadsheet around so that he could see it more clearly. "This was in the database," she explained, "but I printed it out. It makes it easier to follow. I work better with paper and pen," she added.

He wasn't looking at the spreadsheet in question.

He was looking at her. And still frowning. "Yes," he said darkly, "I know."

It wasn't her imagination. There *was* something wrong. She wanted to ask him what it was, but first, she needed to bring this matter to his attention. He needed to be made aware of it.

"I think someone is embezzling from the institute." He looked at her sharply. "Here," Ramona coaxed, "look at this." Pointing to one column on the first page, she then indicated another column on the second sheet. "Somewhere between these two points, this amount of money disappears. And this isn't the only place. It happens several times with different entries. I double-checked the figures, but the totals I come up with don't change." She leaned back in the chair, knowing this had to be hard for him to take in. "I think you're going to need to call in a forensic accountant."

For a moment, Paul wavered, not knowing whether to believe her. If she was right about someone embezzling funds, then this could be disastrous. It was tantamount to one more nail in the institute's coffin.

On the other hand, he reminded himself, this could just be another example of Ramona's artful camouflage, designed to draw all attention away from herself.

He knew what he *wanted* to believe, but that didn't make it true.

Ramona narrowed her eyes. Something was really off. "You don't seem very upset about this," she noted. "Am I wrong?"

That was when she noticed that he was holding a magazine in his hand, rolled up the way someone would when they wanted to kill an annoying insect that crossed their path.

"Have you seen this?"

Paul tossed the magazine on her desk, watching Ramona's face for her reaction. The initial surprise gave way to another expression. Guilt?

His heart froze.

Struggling to keep the extent of his anger under wraps, he pointed at the magazine. "I think you'll be particularly interested in the article beginning on page thirty."

Even before she opened the magazine, Ramona could feel her heart sinking in her chest like a clay pigeon that had been shot down. Her fingers felt almost numb as she turned to the page he told her.

Oh God, he did it. Jessup went ahead and wrote the article after I'd begged him not to.

She didn't have to read the article to know that it was slanted. She could see the truth in Paul's eyes.

How did she make this right?

She took a breath and began to plead her case. "Paul, I can explain—"

Pain shot through him. The last shred of hope that she was actually innocent of this died the second Ramona uttered those words. She *was* responsible.

And everything else that came before, and after, had been a lie.

"I don't want to hear it," he told her coldly, cutting

her off before she could start to weave another web to ensnare him. "I don't want to hear another lie. Just pack up your things and go." He saw her jaw slacken and fall open, but no words emerged. No further lies. "And I wouldn't put the institute on your résumé if I were you," he advised sarcastically. "Because I won't be giving you a letter of recommendation."

Oh God, he was hurt. And it killed her that she was the cause of his pain.

He had to hear her out. She had to make him understand, she thought frantically. "Paul, please, you have to let me explain—"

He couldn't allow it. Because he still cared. Still wanted to believe that this was all a mistake. That she hadn't betrayed him. And if he let her talk, he'd wind up being swayed.

Being made an even bigger fool of than he already was.

"No," he cut her off gruffly. "There's no point. I can't tell the difference between your lies and your half-truths."

"I *wasn't* lying," she cried, desperate to have him understand the situation that had developed. "I mean, I was, but that was only a small part of it. The rest of it, it was all true."

There was pain along with the contempt in his eyes. She was responsible for that. She had to make this right, to turn it around. But now, caught by surprise and shell-shocked, she couldn't even think straight.

"And why would you expect me to believe that?"

he wanted to know. "Just because you say so? I have your word for it, is that it?"

He was mocking her and he had a perfect right to, she thought. All she could do was answer his question as honestly as she could and pray that somehow it would work itself out. That he would believe her. She'd just been trying to do her job and earn some money. She had never planned on falling for him.

"Yes," she cried breathlessly.

"So I have the word of an artful liar," he reviewed coldly. "Is that what you're telling me?"

Every word that he said, every cold look in his eyes slashed at her heart. She reached for him, to make contact, to touch his arm, but he pulled it away. He wanted no part of her, she realized.

"Paul, I didn't—"

"Save your breath, Ramona." And then, to her surprise, he laughed shortly. "At least you gave me your right name, and if I'd had half a brain in my head—because my brother clearly didn't—I would have stopped to look you up on the Internet before ever agreeing to have you stay on."

His mouth curved in a humorless smile. Ramona braced herself. She knew what was coming.

"There were a number of reprinted articles on the Web with your name on them." Scanning them, he'd felt like an idiot. "You're quite the investigative journalist, aren't you?" His eyes narrowed as his mouth hardened. "You must have had a hell of a laugh at my expense."

Oh God, this was getting worse by the second. She would have given anything to undo it, to find just the right thing to say to make him believe her. But she had nothing. Nothing but the truth, which he didn't believe. "I didn't laugh at you, Paul. I never laughed. You opened my eyes—"

"Oh, please," he said dismissively. "Begging doesn't fit your image. By the way, that bit about your mother, that was a really nice touch. You *really* had me going there for a while." When he thought of the time he'd devoted on what amounted to a wild-goose chase… There was a reason he devoted himself to his work instead of socializing. He could depend on medicine. Trusting his instincts when it came to a woman only made him act like a fool. "I even tracked down that so-called sibling."

"Then there *is* one?" Her eyes widened. There was hope, real hope for her mother. At least this was going to turn out right. "Who?" Ramona cried.

"Oh, no." Paul shook his head. He wasn't about to get sucked back into her lies. "I'm not going to have you bothering some stranger just to continue with this charade of yours. Better luck next time," he retorted.

Turning on his heel, Paul walked out. He slammed the door in his wake.

Numb, Ramona stood there, frozen, the slammed door reverberating in her chest.

Chapter Fifteen

He began missing Ramona the moment he told her to leave.

It had been a week now. A week since the article in the medical journal had changed the steady, progressive path he'd been on. Not having Ramona in his life had created a melancholy within him that was becoming a greater and greater burning pain in his gut.

Waking, sleeping—what little he got of it these days—the pain was always there. Haunting him. Reminding him that she was gone.

He'd never gone through this kind of thing before, never cared enough about anyone to hurt the way he did now.

He would have thought, with all the turmoil that Ramona's article had created, that he wouldn't have time to feel anything except outrage. He, Derek and Lisa had all scrambled to release statements to the press that amounted to some very fancy damage control. It seemed to have taken hold and, for now, the furor was beginning to die down again.

Between that, doing a little investigative work of his own and seeing to his patients, two of whom had just discovered that they were finally, *finally* pregnant, he was busy enough this last week for three people.

It didn't matter.

He still missed her. The feeling was a part of everything he did, everything he thought. And a piece of him hoped, however irrationally, that there was some kind of explanation for what had happened. Hoping that the betrayal *wasn't* a betrayal but something else.

Yeah, like what? Face it, buddy, you were played. Now get over it and move on.

Paul knew that *that* would be the right thing to do, the smart thing, to move on with his life. But he just couldn't do it. What was he supposed to move on to? And how?

Sitting at his desk now, he glanced at his calendar. It had been years since he'd had a vacation. Maybe it was time for him to take one. But go where? Do what?

Wherever he went, he would be taking his malaise with him. That wasn't a solution.

It occurred to Paul that he didn't even have a close

friend to turn to, no one to vent to or share these jumbled-up feelings with. Despite the very short time they'd spent together, Ramona had been the one he'd talked to more than anyone, even more than the members of his family. They all expected things of him. She just wanted him to be *him*.

Yeah, right, so she could pull the wool over your eyes.

Enough with this pity party, he upbraided himself. He had work to do. There was no time to behave like a mooning adolescent. He was way too old for that.

Feeling lost and caged at the same time, it took Paul several minutes to realize that he was staring at a folder on his desk that he didn't recognize. Where had it come from? He was fairly certain that he hadn't placed it there, even though the space on his desk was far from orderly this week.

How long had that folder been there?

He was really losing it, Paul thought, dragging a hand through his dark, wayward hair. This *had* to stop. He had to get a grip.

Pulling the folder over, he opened it. Inside were two spreadsheets. He recognized them instantly. They were the ones that Ramona had tried to get him to look at last week. The day he fired her.

His first impulse was to sweep them into the waste-basket. Instead, after a moment of mental wrestling, he began going over the figures.

Ramona had been right, he thought darkly as he continued to review the spreadsheets. The figures *didn't* tally. If she hadn't pointed it out to him, he might have never even noticed the shortfall. He didn't focus on the money end of it beyond making sure that the department was properly funded to provide him with the things he needed to continue his work.

If he had noticed that they were short, he would have just chalked it up to a mistake and corrected it, maybe even funding it out of his own pocket. But the "mistake" occurred in several other places, affecting a number of totals.

Too many to be a coincidence. Someone was playing with the numbers, stealing the money. Why?

Briefly he considered the theory that Ramona was behind this. It could be just another smoke screen she'd set up to divert attention from what she was actually doing. But then he went back to the database where she'd gotten her original figures. Hitting File Stats showed him that no changes had been made to alter the figures during the time that Ramona had been working at the institute.

The data he was looking at had been input by someone else, someone who worked here before Ramona started. Someone who was robbing the institute and had been for what looked like several months now.

Paul stopped and rocked back in his chair, thinking. He was going to have to get someone more knowledgeable than he was to untangle all this and then hopefully track it down to the person who was responsible for the embezzlement.

There was no other word for it. *Embezzlement.*

He wouldn't even have known about this if not for Ramona.

He also wouldn't have been gutted and vivisected if it hadn't been for her, he reminded himself. And he, Derek and Lisa wouldn't have had to scramble to reverse the media's harsh opinion of the institute—and his father—if she hadn't written that damn article.

Oh hell, how stupid could one man be? he berated himself. He'd actually told himself, when he first saw the article, that she couldn't have written it. That she wasn't the type of person who could do something like this. She wouldn't have betrayed and used him this way

Well, obviously, she could and she did and wishing seven ways from sundown that she hadn't would not change a damn thing. *Now* it was time to move on.

He picked up the landline, about to tell his assistant to put a call through to Harvey Nordinger, a discreet accountant who could conduct an audit without arousing anyone's suspicions, when someone knocked on his door.

Paul replaced the receiver. The accounts weren't going anywhere, he'd make the call later. Maybe this was Derek to tell him if there'd been any further progress defusing the volatile situation the accusations in the medical journal had brought about.

Ever the optimist, he thought wearily. "Come in."

* * *

On the other side of the door, Ramona took a deep breath.

Here goes nothing.

Pasting a broad smile on her face, she swung open Paul's door and walked in.

Had she not had an iron backbone, the look on Paul's face would have destroyed her.

"Hello, Paul." She'd thought of addressing him by his formal title, but somehow, calling him "Dr. Armstrong" seemed artificial, especially after the moments—hours—they'd shared.

She did her best not to focus on the last part.

For a split second, when he saw Ramona in the doorway, his heart had skipped a beat. But then the memory of how she'd lied to him, how she'd used him, kicked in with the force of an angry mule.

It didn't help. He still cared about her.

Damn it, why was she here? He was too vulnerable to see her now—because he knew he wanted her badly enough to forgive her anything.

He couldn't have her talking her way back into his life. Not until he could think clearly.

"Get out," he told her.

Rather than comply, Ramona calmly looked at him and said, "No, I won't." Just before she turned around and locked the door. "Not until you hear me out." Taking the key out of the lock, she underscored her statement by slipping the key down the front of her blouse.

Did she think he wouldn't go after the key there? Or was she hoping he would? "That's a little melodramatic, don't you think?"

"Maybe." She patted the region between her breasts, pushing the key against her skin. "But I also know you're gentleman enough not to try to retrieve it."

His eyes narrowed as he envisioned the key's hiding place. "Don't count on it," he warned.

Actually, there was very little she wanted as much as having his hands on her right now. The only thing that trumped that was the desire to make him listen to her—that and getting him to forgive her.

She shook her head. "I know you better than you know yourself." She took an envelope from her purse and placed it on his desk.

He eyed it, but made no attempt to reach for the envelope. It remained where she'd placed it. "What's this?"

"A signed and dated statement from my mother's doctor that he diagnosed her with leukemia six months ago." Why wasn't he picking up the envelope? Did he think it was a trick? "Dr. Richard Sanger is one of the best oncologists in the state." She raised her eyes to his. "If you don't believe him, I also brought along a copy of my mother's lab work. It's all there."

This time, the envelope she took out of her oversize purse was a thick manila one that made a small *thud* when she dropped it on his desk.

"I wasn't lying to you. My mother *is* seriously ill

and she *does* need a bone-marrow transplant. I took this assignment because I needed the money and because I needed to find out if she had any other children I could reach out to." She took a breath, trying to subdue the building panic she felt. "I don't have much time."

She was handing him the proof on a silver platter. The last of his unfounded hope splintered. "So you did write the article in that journal."

"No," she insisted. "My editor wrote it. When he called to see how far along I was and I told him I'd only taken photographs of the files, he made me send him the photographs and my notes. I told him I'd only do that if he didn't have someone else write the article. I also told him I needed time to separate fact from rumor. He gave me his word he wouldn't have anyone else write it." Anger entered her voice as she continued. "Technically, he pointed out when I called him on this, he'd kept his word. He wrote the article himself."

Paul's frown deepened. "Potato, po-tah-to," he concluded sarcastically.

Ramona laughed shortly. "That's what I said to him when I gave him back his advance—and quit."

That surprised him. "You quit?"

She knew he wouldn't believe her. That was why she'd brought proof. "You want to see the letter of resignation?" As she asked, she began digging through her purse. "I can't work for someone I can't trust."

Getting up, Paul rounded his desk and put his hand

on hers, bringing her search to an end. "That won't be necessary. I believe you."

Suspicion, created out of fear, warred with relief. She raised her eyes to his again, searching to see if he was telling her the truth. "Why now?"

"Because you were right about there being monetary discrepancies. Because I've already called around, making inquiries, and found out that your mother's on the transplant list." It had taken calling in a string of favors, something he'd never done before. It had also taken bending a few rules, something else he'd never done before. But this was for a woman who, God help him, he loved.

She would have rather that he'd believed her on his own, without searching for proof, but she couldn't exactly blame him, seeing as how she had come to work here with a hidden agenda, determined to substantiate the rumors about unethical practices conducted at the institute.

Renewed hope suddenly flourished through her. "Does that mean that you'll give me the name of my mother's child?"

"I don't know the name," he told her, and her heart sank. "But I do know the name of the family."

Paul was being literal, she realized. He'd thought that she was asking him for a first name. That was only of secondary importance. Where she could find this sibling was what came first.

"Oh, thank God. What is it?"

First things first, he schooled himself. "Before I tell you that, I have to tell you that you might have been right."

Thoughts were swirling in and out of her head, making it hard for her to concentrate. Making it even harder to follow what he was saying without some kind of cue card. "About what?"

"About misconduct going on. Not now," he quickly amended because he didn't want her to think that he was in any way responsible for it, "but during the years when my father ran things."

This wasn't easy for him. There was no love lost between Paul and his father, but he'd always had the utmost respect for the man as a physician and as a pioneer in his field. What Gerald Armstrong had done to up his success rate, to forge a reputation as being *the* person to come to in order to solve infertility problems, cast a dark shadow across all his true accomplishments.

"From what I could ascertain, the recipient of your mother's 'donation,'" Paul said delicately, "had no knowledge that her own eggs weren't being used. According to the records, the recipient couldn't produce healthy, viable eggs. But she had been adamant about having my father use her eggs along with her husband's sperm to create an embryo. From what I saw in my father's notes, he knew if he did, the procedure was doomed to failure. So he made a substitution without telling either her or her husband. The result," he told her, "produced a little girl—and a great many generous monetary donations to the institute over the years."

She only wanted to know one thing. "And their name is?"

He hesitated for only a moment, his dedication to the patient's right to privacy warring with his desire to possibly save the life of her mother. Life won out over privacy.

"Welsh. Hayden and Estelle Welsh."

Her eyes widened as the information sank in. "The New York Welshes?" she cried, stunned. "As in richer-than-Rockefeller Hayden and Estelle Welsh?"

Paul nodded. "The very same."

She closed her eyes for a moment, both overjoyed to finally discover that she had a sibling, someone who might be able to save her mother, and at the same time significantly daunted—because approaching this young woman who had grown up believing that Estelle Welsh was her biological mother was not going to be easy. The young woman had absolutely no idea about her real origins. Most likely, she would think she was being lied to for financial gain.

But to save her mother's life, Ramona was more than willing to walk through the very gates of hell if she had to. Cornering an heiress should be a cakewalk in comparison.

"Thank you," Ramona said with sincerity. She knew that telling her had to cost him. He had gone against his principles. "Thank you for tracking all this down for me—for my mother," she amended, since she had a feeling he was still angry at her for her initial deception. For not trusting him enough to be honest from the start.

She couldn't read the expression on his face. Was he still angry, or had he gone on to indifference? She wasn't sure which was worse.

Taking a breath, she knew she couldn't leave until she told him everything. "I just want you to know, I never meant to hurt you. And I never meant to fall in love with you," she added in a much lower voice, saying it almost to herself. "It just happened."

A flicker of surprise came and went from his eyes, but he gave no other indication that he had even heard her. "There's more," he told her.

Ramona's face lit up with hope. "More siblings?" she asked eagerly.

She'd misunderstood, he thought. "No. But I managed to pull a few strings." He wasn't about to go into any detail as to what favors he'd called in. That was for him to know, not her. "Your mother's at the top of the recipients list now."

Tears instantly filled her eyes as Ramona steepled her fingers before her lips to keep the sobs back. Pulling herself together, she murmured a heartfelt, if perforce, very quiet "Thank you." Blinking back tears, she reached down her blouse into her bra and drew out the key she'd hidden. She held it out to him. "I guess you'll be wanting this now."

He took the key from her. Contact with her skin had

made the metal warm. Paul closed his fingers around it, savoring the heat.

"There's no hurry," he told her. "The door can stay locked a little while longer."

A ray of sunshine stirred inside her. She told herself not to entertain any false hopes. But, being the optimist she was, she couldn't help it. "Oh?"

He answered her question with a question of his own. "Were you serious just then?"

"I was completely serious about everything I said," Ramona told him solemnly. "What part are you referring to?"

There was a hint of a smile on his lips. "The part where you said you fell in love with me."

Had she made a mistake, letting that slip out? Paul probably felt as if she was putting him on the spot, cornering him. "I'm sorry. I didn't mean to make you feel uncomfortable—"

His eyes held hers as he cut her off. "Did I say I was uncomfortable?"

"No, but—" This time she was the one who stopped herself abruptly. "Paul, where is this going?" She knew where she wanted it to go, but she couldn't read her own feelings into his words. It would be too disappointing when she turned out to be wrong.

"I don't know yet," he admitted, measuring his words out slowly. "I've never been in this kind of situation before." Sitting on the edge of his desk, he put his hands on her hips and drew her to him. "Although, when two people feel like this about each other, it usually ends with some kind of ceremony," he theorized, and then added, "generally a wedding."

Ramona's mouth fell open.

She'd come here to try to convince him to forgive her. This was something she hadn't even contemplated because she felt it was too far out of her reach. "A wedding?" she echoed.

He was going too fast, Paul thought. But that was because he had no experience with this. The proper way to conduct a relationship, the proper way to do *anything* with a woman was really out of his realm of expertise.

"I'm not rushing you," he assured her quickly. "We'll take it one step at a time. But I want to warn you that I mean to do everything in my power to convince you to say yes." The more he talked about it, the more right it felt to him. "Being with you made me see that the world comes in colors, not just black and white. I want you with me forever, Ramona, so that I never take myself so seriously that I forget why I'm doing all this again."

She couldn't begin to find a word for the way she felt, but *stunned* would have to do until she came up with something better.

Her head was spinning. "Are you asking me to marry you?"

"Yes. No," he said almost immediately after he'd said yes. "Eventually," he finally amended. "When you get used to the idea."

Ramona grinned and her eyes began to shine. "I'm used to it," she declared.

He'd expected that convincing her to marry him was going to take a few months, not a few seconds. "Really?"

"Really," she murmured just before she offered up her mouth to his.

He took the hint instantly.

* * * * *

Don't miss the next chapter in the new
Special Edition continuity,
THE BABY CHASE.
Olivia Armstrong made the perfect match
when she married junior senator
Jamison Mallory. The only thing missing
from their picture-perfect life is
the baby they both desire.
Will the Armstrong Fertility Institute
be the answer?
Don't miss
THE FAMILY THEY CHOSE
by
Nancy Robards Thompson.
On sale February 2010,
wherever Silhouette Books are sold.

*Fan favorite Leslie Kelly is bringing her
readers a fantasy so scandalous,
we're calling it FORBIDDEN!*

*Look for
PLAY WITH ME
Available February 2010
from Harlequin® Blaze™.*

"AREN'T YOU GOING TO SAY 'Fly me' or at least 'Welcome aboard'?"

Amanda Bauer didn't. The softly muttered word that actually came out of her mouth was a lot less welcoming. And had fewer letters. Four, to be exact.

The man shook his head and tsked. "Not exactly the friendly skies. Haven't caught the spirit yet this morning?"

"Make one more airline-slogan crack and you'll be walking to Chicago," she said.

He nodded once, then pushed his sunglasses onto the top of his tousled hair. The move revealed blue eyes that matched the sky above. And yeah. They were twinkling. Damn it.

"Understood. Just, uh, promise me you'll say 'Coffee, tea or me' at least once, okay? Please?"

Amanda tried to glare, but that twinkle sucked the annoyance right out of her. She could only draw in a slow breath as he climbed into the plane. As she watched her passenger disappear into the small jet, she had to wonder about the trip she was about to take.

Coffee and tea they had, and he was welcome to them. But her? Well, she'd never even considered making a move on a customer before. Talk about unprofessional.

And yet…

Something inside her suddenly wanted to take a chance, to be a little outrageous.

How long since she had done indecent things—or decent ones, for that matter—with a sexy man? Not since before they'd thrown all their energies into expanding Clear-Blue Air, at the very least. She hadn't had time for a lunch date, much less the kind of lustfest she'd enjoyed in her younger years. The kind that lasted for entire weekends and involved not leaving a bed except to grab the kind of sensuous food that could be smeared onto—and eaten off—someone else's hot, naked, sweat-tinged body.

She closed her eyes, her hand clenching tight on the railing. Her heart fluttered in her chest and she tried to make herself move. But she couldn't—not climbing up, but not backing away, either. Not physically, and not in her head.

Was she really considering this? God, she hadn't even looked at the stranger's left hand to make sure he was available. She had no idea if he was actually attracted to her or just an irrepressible flirt. Yet something inside was telling her to take a shot with this man.

It was crazy. Something she'd never considered. Yet right now, at this moment, she was definitely considering it. If he was available…could she do it? Seduce a stranger. Have an anonymous fling, like something out of a blue movie on late-night cable?

She didn't know. All she knew was that the flight to Chicago was a short one so she had to decide quickly. And as she put her foot on the bottom step and began to climb up, Amanda suddenly had to wonder if she was about to embark on the ride of her life.

HARLEQUIN® *Blaze*™

It all started
with a few naughty books....

As a member of the Red Tote Book Club, Carol Snow has been studying works of classic erotic literature...but Carol doesn't believe in love...or marriage. It's going to take another kind of classic—Charles Dickens's *A Christmas Carol*—and a little otherworldly persuasion to convince her to go after her own sexily ever after.

Cuddle up with

Her Sexy Valentine
by STEPHANIE BOND

Available February 2010

---

red-hot reads

www.eHarlequin.com

HB79526

REQUEST YOUR FREE BOOKS!

2 FREE NOVELS PLUS 2 FREE GIFTS!

Silhouette

SPECIAL EDITION

Life, Love and Family!

SSE10

HARLEQUIN
Ambassadors

*Want to share your passion
for reading Harlequin® Books?*

Become a Harlequin Ambassador!

Harlequin Ambassadors are a group
of passionate and well-connected readers
who are willing to share their joy of reading
Harlequin® books with family and friends.

You'll be sent all the tools you need to spark
great conversation, including free books!

All we ask is that you share the romance
with your friends and family!

You'll also be invited to have a say in
new book ideas and exchange opinions
with women just like you!

**To see if you qualify* to be
a Harlequin Ambassador, please visit
www.HarlequinAmbassadors.com.**

Thank you for your participation.